2030

Martin Chu Shui

Author: Chu Shui, Martin, 1962 –

Title: 2036

ISBN: 9798693141995

Prologue

A guy is inside an enclosed room, and there are two slits on the wall; one opens to the inside, and the other to the outside. When a piece of paper is pushed through the in-slit, the guy's instructions are to find a shape-matching piece of paper from a pile of paper inside the room and then push it out through the out-slit. Despite the seemingly random squiggles on the paper that don't mean anything to him, by following the instructions, he performs his duty perfectly.

The squiggles on the paper are in fact questions and answers written in Chinese, so from an outsider's viewpoint, this guy is proficient in the Chinese language and capable of understanding and answering questions in Chinese. It's called "Chinese Room" in artificial consciousness terms.

Part One

1.   Underground Car Park

Olivia walked hurriedly along the street among high-rise buildings in Sydney's Central Business District. She had just finished a psychological appraisal session with a corporate client. She typed impatiently on the Ixis sticking to her wrist, still not seeing any taxis coming her way. Looking up and staring at the mid-air traffic, Olivia sighed; Friday after-work rush hour.

It was May, supposedly the cooler season for Sydney, but the last time Olivia felt cool outside of permanently air-conditioned buildings was over fifteen years ago when she was still in high school. Sydney's winter season seemed all but completely disappeared; the temperature hovered around forty degrees Celsius during the day and merely dropped to around thirty after sunset. However, it was not too bad at the moment. Thanks to the unseasonal stormy weather during the last few days, the city had cooled down quite significantly. As a result, city dwellers had flocked out to enjoy the rare cooler outdoor experience. Olivia found it fascinating to watch their facial expressions. They took such pure enjoyment from such a basic and simple activity. It was so contagious that she decided to forget about trying to get a taxi and just walk home.

The dirty streets, lit by pale streetlights and the illumination from advertising signs, felt deserted, despite crowds of people everywhere. Her best friend and roommate, Zoe, would be back this weekend from her months-long business trip in Africa. Olivia had promised Zoe that she would pick her up from the airport. She would also like to organize a gathering with their friends from their university era, Ava and Sophie, a sort of welcome home party for Zoe, but the question was where. None of their apartments were ideal, not only because they were too small, but also because of Ava and Sophie's "boyfriends." They

3

could try their usual venue, Rose café, on the ground floor of the tallest building in Sydney, a trendy place one must be seen at. They could also listen to popular band Glass Box's live performance there, but to be honest, she was getting a bit tired of it recently. They needed to find somewhere new, something exciting. Olivia couldn't remember the last time she'd had a face-to-face meeting with either Ava or Sophie; based on their regular phone conversations, they were quite involved with their so-called "boyfriends" and always "extremely busy" during after-work hours. Although she would never get involved with the kind of "boyfriends" her friends had, Olivia did envy them from time to time. She felt lonely, particularly during the past couple of months while Zoe was not here...

Olivia was completely immersed in her own thoughts. Lifting up her gaze, she suddenly realized that she was almost home. Just then, she noticed a young homeless man who sat under a closed shop-front doorway. He stared at her with an intensity that worried her, particularly when the young man suddenly stood up and moved toward her very fast, in a manner that was really worrisome. Olivia couldn't help but break into a run, quickly leaving the scene.

Olivia was quite fit due to her regular exercise regimen, and this was her territory; she knew every corner of the streets like the back of her own hands. Her apartment was only a few blocks away, so while running through the crowd, Olivia was not panicked at all, even after seeing the young man was running after her.

After turning around a street corner, Olivia stopped, looking back; the homeless man was nowhere to be seen. She breathed out in relief and turned, walking at a more leisurely pace toward home.

Olivia bumped into someone. It was like running into a brick wall. Olivia felt pain in her shoulder. Before she was able to see whom she had bumped into and well before she had opened her mouth to apologize, a large hand covered her mouth; a bag was hurriedly pulled over her head.

The man's grip was so strong that Olivia was unable to struggle at all; all she could manage to do was tremble continuously. Olivia's mind went completely blank. She'd never had such an experience in her whole life, and she couldn't think at all. She felt like she was being dragged off the street into a nearby building, then she sensed that they were inside an elevator and moving downward for a while. Finally, she was dragged out of the elevator and the bag over her head was removed.

Olivia blinked her eyes a few times, focused on her surroundings, and found she was in an empty parking lot. There were five thugs around her, all tall and big. They looked like military guys with short haircuts, but they were wearing casual civilian clothes. She felt like her limbs were frozen, unable to move at all.

"Look what we got here: a human girl. I haven't touched a human female for a while," the shortest thug said.

Although the initial shockwaves were still humming through Olivia's body, she was surprised that she had actually calmed down a bit; at least her body had stopped trembling. She examined the thugs more closely; the other four thugs were taller and bigger than the one who had just spoken, and their faces remained emotionless. Olivia was sure she had bumped into one of these guys.

There was nobody in sight, just a couple of cars parked in the far corner. She needed help, to alert someone to her situation, so without one moment's delay, Olivia started screaming at the top of her voice with all of her strength. After a while longer, Olivia stopped, feeling exhausted.

None of the thugs tried to stop her. The shorter thug spoke with a grin on his face while the others remained expressionless. "I like your screaming; it turns me on, but you'd better save some energy so we can have a good time together."

Watching the evil grin on the thug's ugly face, Olivia felt scared and desperate. Please, someone, hear me and come to my aid, she thought. Then she screamed again, but at a much lower volume and with less energy. Finally, she collapsed on the ground and sobbed helplessly.

"You can scream the whole night, but nobody will come to help you," the shorter thug said. He seemed in no hurry to do anything except stand there and enjoy himself, as if watching a show.

"Please don't hurt me...I don't want to die..." Olivia begged as she sobbed.

"Keep begging; it turns me on even more than your screaming. I won't hurt you, and I guarantee we'll have a good time together," said the shorter thug.

By now, Olivia found that she was able to think again. There were reports about a series of murders of young women in the past few months, but they had all happened in the suburbs on the outskirts of the city. She would never have imagined that this could happen to her with so many people on the streets. Looking at the large knives on their belts visible through their open jackets, Olivia knew the truth: she would not survive tonight.

It felt strange even to herself after realizing her fate, but Olivia actually calmed down completely and felt relief. She was no longer scared. Closing her eyes, she could see Leo's face in her mind: his kind eyes, his witty jokes, his lovely grin. Olivia could even sense a trace of sadness on his handsome face, as if he didn't want to see her so soon.

"Leo, I miss you so much. I'll see you soon," Olivia murmured. Then she heard a calm voice.

"Let her go!"

Olivia was shocked. It was Leo's voice, but that was impossible. Was she imagining things because she was facing

6

her own death? Olivia was afraid to open her eyes to find out the truth. Even if it was only her imagination, she wanted it to last as long as possible. It gave her some comfort in her desperate situation, even if it was only a delusion. A few short moments passed, but nothing happened. With great reluctance, Olivia forced herself to open her eyes. She saw the young homeless man who had chased her earlier standing in front of these thugs.

Feeling disappointed and sorry for this young man, she cried, "Please go away and leave me alone. I don't want you getting hurt too."

"Let her go!" the young man repeated calmly while staring at the thugs.

"You should listen to her and leave, but I wouldn't let you go anyway," the short thug said.

The young man didn't move. "I'll let you live if you leave now."

"I am so scared," laughed the shorter thug. He then signalled the other thugs. "Kill him!"

Olivia stared at what was happening in front of her in total horror: the four thugs launched themselves at the young man. They were fast, and they looked like they were well trained; soon they surrounded the young man.

The young man seemed very calm. He fought with the four thugs furiously. The struggle was fast and violent; blood splashed out as punches tore wounds on their bodies.

"Don't kill him. I want to capture him alive," ordered the shorter thug.

Although the young man fought strongly, his opponents were too many and too strong for him to deal with. He knelt down after a heavy blow to his stomach. Olivia couldn't help but scream out loud as a thug used his large knife's blunt handle to knock the back of the young man's head.

7

The young man fell to the ground. Just as Olivia thought it would be the end of him—and her—she was astonished to see him bounce up immediately. Like an enraged lion, inhuman roars came out of his mouth; blood from his head injury soaked the back of his shirt. His fighting style suddenly changed, so unfamiliar to Olivia that she assumed it was some kind of Kung Fu.

The young man moved rapidly in circles, so fast and agile that his opponents' attacks always missed him at the last moment. Rather than using his fists, he used the edges of his palms, chopping at the thugs.

The situation changed immediately. The young man used his palm to chop one thug on the back of his neck and struck another in his throat; both fell on the ground, still.

"What the hell is this? Kill him." Withdrawing his large military knife, the shorter thug joined the battle.

Three large blades shone under the pale lights of the parking lot, slashing at the young man. Olivia screamed after a few cuts found the young man's arms and legs. He ran away from the crowd, and the thugs pursued closely.

The young man suddenly turned sideways, twisting his body and gripping the first thug's wrist; with a slick manoeuvre, the large knife was in his hand. It seemed like a smooth and continuous movement: gripping the wrist, taking over the knife, and slicing it through the thug's throat.

Before Olivia could make any sound or the remaining two thugs were able to react, the young man stretched his arm, making a large curve. As blood spilled into mid-air, the other two thugs fell to the ground with heavy thudding sounds.

It suddenly became silent, deadly silent, literally. Olivia stared at the bodies of the dead thugs scattered over the parking lot, lying still in their own blood. It felt so unreal, as if she was in a nightmare. Turning, she saw the young man had fallen to the ground. He struggled to a sitting position and tore strips from his own clothes to cover his wounds. Only then was Olivia jolted back to her senses; she quickly walked over and helped him to bandage his wounds to stop the bleeding.

"Are they all dead?" he asked. The wild expression on his face made her scared; he looked like a wounded wild animal.

Olivia nodded.

The expression on his face changed to relief; he breathed out deeply.

"I'm calling the police and an ambulance now..." Olivia tapped her wrist while speaking but he said urgently, "No police, no ambulance, no authority. Please." He paused and asked curiously, "Why are you tapping your wrist?"

"I am making the phone call...never mind," said Olivia. "Okay, I won't make the call. Are you able to walk?" She wouldn't be able to carry his large body.

He nodded.

"My apartment is very close to here. Would you like to come to my place so we can get you fixed up?" asked Olivia. She felt uneasy inviting a stranger to her apartment, but under the circumstances she knew she had no choice.

He nodded again.

"I am Olivia. What's your name?"

"Nice to meet you, Olivia. I am..." A shocked expression suddenly appeared on his face. "I can't remember my name."

2. Stay

Olivia looked at him very worriedly; the heavy blow to the back of his head might have damaged his memory. They'd need to leave here and get to her apartment first. She went over and stripped the long overcoat from one of the dead thugs. Thankfully it was clear of blood. She helped the nameless young man to put the coat on to cover his blood-covered body. Olivia put his arm around her shoulder and then helped him to slowly walk out of the parking lot.

Olivia helped inside her apartment and laid him on the couch in the living area. As if he had used up his last drop of energy, he fell asleep as soon as his head touched the couch. Olivia hoped nobody saw him on their way up.

"Dinner for two tonight, miss?" her oven asked.

"Shut up! I don't need dinner," said Olivia.

"No need to be so rude. I would also like to remind you to get his food ration coupons, because men can eat a lot," said the oven.

"Sorry, but I am busy right now. First aid, come here," Olivia ordered.

Soon a box walked over to her on its four legs. "What can I do for you, my lady?"

"Not me, him." Olivia pointed at the nameless young man lying on her couch, fast sleep.

A beam of blue light issued from the box and scanned the young man's body a few times. "Despite quite a lot of blood covering his body, the wounds on his arms and legs are quite superficial, but the injury on the back of his head is most worrying. It could have potentially damaged his brain or caused memory loss."

"Tell me something I don't know." Olivia wasn't in a good mood. She paused and then said, "Tell me what I should do first."

Olivia used wet towels to wipe the blood from his face and then stared at the blood-soaked bandages. She had no idea where to start.

"Miss, you'll need to take the bandages off and redress the wound," said the first aid box.

"I know bloody well I have to do that, it's just I haven't done such a thing before." Olivia contemplated how to handle the tasks ahead of her.

"I'd suggest using a pair of sterilized scissors to cut the old bandages off. Here are the scissors, miss." A pair of medical scissors was handed over by the first aid box.

"I haven't done such a thing before. What happens if I cut his skin by mistake? What should I do if I cause the wound to start bleeding again?" Olivia stared at the scissors, very afraid to pick them up.

Maybe Olivia and the medical box's conversation woke him up, but the young man opened his eyes, looking at Olivia and then the box with the scissors held in its outstretched mechanical arm. "Please don't worry about redressing my wound. Just let me sleep and I'll be all right tomorrow morning." After that, he went back to sleep again.

"Miss, I'd strongly suggest you redress the wound before it gets infected…" Olivia interrupted the box by putting her index finger on her lips.

"Shush. Go back where you came from, now!" she said quietly but firmly. "And be quiet!" she added.

The medical box shook its arm as if shaking its head and slowly and quietly re-packed itself, then walked soundlessly out of the living area.

In the dark, Olivia sat against the couch, watching him sleep soundly. She thought about her life as a single woman for the last five years and how weird it felt to have a man sleeping on her couch.

Olivia first met Leo ten years ago when she was still an eighteen-year-old university student. She could still remember clearly the first moment she lay eyes on him. She went to a free evening lecture about artificial consciousness. Olivia wasn't keen on the topic and was dragged there by her then-roommate. She told her roommate that she'd stay there a maximum of fifteen minutes and would walk straight out. Of course, after seeing the speaker—Leo, then a PhD student—Olivia not only stayed for the whole two-hour lecture but also attended every single one of his public speeches in the six months after that. Later, after they were involved, Leo told her that he noticed her on her first appearance during his speech. Olivia would never forget how sweet and lovely Leo was; memories of the time they spent together flooded back, making her smile. They both believed they had finally found their true soul mate. But. There's always a but. Olivia shook her head bitterly. Her boyfriend, her true love, was killed in an accident five years ago, almost exactly five years after they first met each other.

After Leo's death, she had been through regular psychological therapy up until recently. Almost everyone around her, including her psychologist, told her that she was still in the denial stage of her grieving process and needed to move on, but she had no interest in any male. Her family members and friends had tried to get her to meet with other guys, and she politely declined them all. Later, her friends suggested she should get a Taibot boyfriend like most of them, and she thought that was an even more stupid idea.

A few months after Leo's death, Zoe suggested sharing an apartment with her in Sydney CBD. Olivia knew that Zoe did this purely for her benefit, because Zoe had no need to spend money renting such an expensive apartment in central Sydney; she travelled overseas most of the time and only spent a few days in Sydney occasionally, so she could easily stay with her family. Olivia did appreciate Zoe's generous help and real friendship. In fact, all of her friends from her university years, like Sophie, Ava, and many others, were very helpful.

Despite what everyone else told her consistently, despite the fact she knew it sounded ridiculous, somehow, deep down in her heart, Olivia felt that Leo was still alive somewhere. Leo worked as a researcher in an artificial intelligent laboratory when the fatal accident happened, but she hadn't been told what happened to his body. It might have been cremated or buried; she had no idea. More strangely, she was unable to find out, since the accident was a highly classified national security matter. She shook her head and sighed; everyone else might be right and she might still be in denial about Leo's death.

Listening to his even breathing, Olivia couldn't believe that she could be attracted to this stranger, a nameless young man she knew nothing about. Maybe it was because when she first heard his voice, it sounded like Leo's, or more likely it was because he had saved her life.

Olivia swore that his voice sounded exactly like Leo's when she heard it with her eyes closed the very first time, but later, after seeing the voice owner's face, she had difficulty associating Leo with this stranger. It could well be that when she was facing death, her brain played a trick on her. Working as a corporate psychological consultant, Olivia knew about these kinds of mind tricks very well.

Olivia stared at the young man in the darkness; how could he fight like that and kill the five big, strong, and armed thugs? How did he know that strange Kung Fu style? Why didn't he want to contact the police or authorities? When this thought burst into her mind, Olivia shuddered: could he be a criminal? Or was he on the most wanted list of some government?

No, there was no way he could be a criminal, not with the way he fought in order to save her life. So the alternative would be that he could be a secret agent, like Zoe. Maybe he was on a secret mission for the UK government. That made sense, since he had a British accent. That would explain how he was able to fight like that and kill the thugs. Yes, that was more likely the case.

It was a big relief to solve the mystery. Olivia felt much better. With that thought fixed in her mind, she fell asleep sitting against the couch.

Olivia opened her eyes and smiled at the wonderful smell of coffee. He was already up, looking showered and shaved, and had also helped himself to Leo's clothes, which were still hanging in her wardrobe. For a brief moment, she thought it was Leo standing in front of her.

He put a tray of breakfast and a mug of coffee on the coffee table beside her. She was confused and unable to speak for a while. Finally, she said, "How do you feel?"

"I am fine," he said casually.

Olivia looked at him in great disbelief; the wound on the back of his head was gone. The hair over the wound was washed and looked shiny. She wondered if the wounds on his arms and legs were healed as well. Just then, her phone rang, and her mother appeared on her whole-wall TV screen. It was fortunate her mother was unable to see her apartment because she rarely enabled the image function on her phone. She didn't have time to deal with her mother right now, so Olivia typed on her wrist to turn her phone off.

"Is the thin film sticking to your wrist a phone?" asked the nameless young man.

"You don't know that?" Olivia asked, surprised. "Yes, it's a phone. I remember you asking the same question last night. So you don't know it because you lost your memories?"

"I don't know."

14

Olivia thought about it for a while and then said, "The wound on the back of your head has gone. How could you recover so quickly?"

"I don't know. This morning when I woke up, I had a shower, and everything seems fine," he said.

Olivia nodded. The answer could be part of his lost memory. Then she felt a pang of fear as a thought came into her mind, but she kept telling herself that it was not possible. "Can you remember anything before the fight last night?"

He shook his head. "I can only remember from the moment I found you in the underground parking lot. I have no memories before that."

"I suppose you have no idea how you were able to fight like that and kill the five thugs." She continued after he nodded. "I gave this a lot of thoughts last night: you could be a secret agent working for the UK government, and that'd explain your excellent fighting abilities."

"On the other hand, I could be a wanted criminal," he said.

Olivia liked his sense of humour, which reminded her of Leo somehow. She told herself that she had to try to forget about Leo, at least in front of this young man. She shook her head. "No, you are not a criminal, not after the way you risked your life to save mine."

"I don't know." The expression on his face showed his frustration.

"Please don't push yourself too hard. Just relax, and your memories might come back soon." Olivia picked up the coffee mug, took a sip and smiled. She hadn't tasted such perfectly made coffee since Leo passed away; Leo was the only one able to make it. No, she had to switch her mind away from Leo, Olivia reminded herself again. "Did you or the machine make this coffee?"

"I don't like coffee from machines. It lacks character." He sat on the couch beside her.

Yes, that was Leo's usual line. What was wrong with her? Why did she associate everything he said and did with Leo? Olivia decided to go back to the most important issue. "Let's assume you are not a wanted criminal; do you have any idea why you don't want to contact the police or authorities?"

"There could be many possibilities, but it's almost meaningless to talk about them," he said.

Olivia carefully chose her words. "My roommate, Zoe, is a secret field agent working for the Australian government. She may be able to help you out."

"Your roommate? Where is she now?"

"She is in Africa at the moment but will be back tomorrow night."

He seemed to think about her proposal for a while and then shook his head. "No, I don't want to get involved with any kind of authorities. I don't know why."

Olivia thought about it for a long time and then made up her mind. "Last night, if you hadn't fought the thugs, I would have died for sure, and you lost your memories as a result. I don't care if you are a wanted criminal. I want to help you and protect you." She paused, staring into his eyes for a second, and then continued. "Stay here with me until you recover your memories; otherwise, it could be very dangerous for you to go out. Someone could be out there looking for you and trying to hurt you."

Olivia smiled after seeing him nod.

"Sorry for taking them without asking." He indicated the clothes he wore.

Olivia shook her head. "No problem. They fit you perfectly."

"Are they your boyfriend's?"

Olivia nodded.

"Did he leave you?"

"No," Olivia said quietly. "He died in an accident."

"I am sorry."

16

"It's okay." Olivia sipped some of her coffee. She could see the genuine apologetic and sympathetic expression on his face; it made her feel reassured. "What should I call you, since you can't remember your own name?"

"Hang on." He seemed to suddenly remember something.

Olivia thought his memory had somehow recovered, but her hope faded as he disappeared into the bathroom. She didn't have to wait long before he returned. Olivia looked at him expectantly.

He put his hand forward; a piece of thin film was lying on his palm. "I found this stuck on my wrist this morning when I had a shower. It must be my phone. You may be able to find out something about me from it."

Olivia cursed herself internally. How could she miss such a basic thing last night? Well, it was a very traumatic event. How could she be expected to pay attention to what was on his wrist with so much blood on his body? Anyway, that didn't matter now.

Olivia put her wrist over the thin film and typed on her wrist a few times; the contents of the film were displayed on her whole-wall TV screen.

3.   Africa

"What time is our flight?" Zoe stared at the endless stream of refugees walking along the dusty road. It was supposedly the rainy season in North Africa, but there hadn't been a drop of rain in this part of the world for the last five years.

"Ten tonight," Nick answered.

Zoe glanced at her wrist. "That's almost eight hours away. Why did we leave so early?"

"Because of these people, my lady." The captain, who sat in the passenger seat, turned to Zoe, gesturing at the endless crowd outside of their military jeep.

"I am sorry..." Zoe mumbled.

"You should be! Thanks to the pollution you westerners created, global warming destroyed our homeland. Do you know how many people died just last year?"

"Approximately fifty million died from starvation and malnutrition in Africa last year, but nobody knows the exact number because..."

"It's a rhetorical question; he doesn't need an answer," Zoe said to Nick.

"Yes, I do, my lady." The captain gazed into Zoe's eyes. "You westerners pumped greenhouse gases into the atmosphere for hundreds of years to gain your wealth, but it is the innocent people, my people, who have to pay the price. Do you know that the famine is so bad that people have started eating the dead? Do you know how many of them have never used electricity in their whole life?"

"I don't have exact data for that question..."

"Shut up, Nick," Zoe said. "We are all very sorry for what is happening here. It was the biggest mistake human civilization ever made. But we have gotten rid of most fossil fuels in our society..."

"That's not good enough," the captain interrupted. "Rich countries like yours need to help our people to survive at least, to redeem your mistakes."

"We have tried our best to help, but we hardly even produce enough food for ourselves," Zoe said quietly.

"Of course you can't. You have not only killed my people but your own people as well. Very soon we will all be doomed; the human race will be terminated." The captain kept his gaze on Zoe's face.

Zoe turned her head away, avoiding the captain's eyes, staring at the people walking under the scorching sunlight. Her eyes met a young mother's, who was holding a baby and walking just outside of her window. The jeep was moving at the same speed as the crowd. Zoe smiled at the young mother, who smiled back, then suddenly collapsed.

"Stop the car!" Zoe shouted.

"What's the matter, my lady?" said the captain.

"She just collapsed, and she had a baby in her arms." Zoe pointed outside the window.

"People are dying everywhere." The captain didn't even look out of the car. "You can't help everyone…"

Zoe opened the door and jumped out of the slow-moving vehicle. She tried to squeeze through the refugee crowd, trying to reach the young women. She didn't get very far before the captain and Nick caught up with her. The dozen soldiers who sat in the back of the military truck leading her jeep also quickly surrounded Zoe to form a protective circle.

"Do you have a death wish?" shouted the captain.

"I can't let her die in front of my eyes. She can have my food and water," Zoe shouted back.

"If you westerners had thought about others a bit earlier, these people wouldn't be suffering now." The captain paused and then said, "Please get back to the car. You will be torn to pieces if you stay in the crowd alone."

"Do they really hate us that much?" asked Zoe.

"Millions of people have already died and millions more are dying. Would you blame them for hating westerners like you who caused all of this in the first place? I would have killed you myself if I had not been ordered to protect you. Nick, get your master into the jeep, now!" shouted the captain again.

"Please let me just give her some food and water," said Zoe.

The captain nodded reluctantly.

Under the escort of dozens of soldiers, Zoe walked to the young woman. She held the woman's head against her chest and fed her some water. Slowly the young woman opened her eyes and said something to Zoe. Nick translated.

"Thank you so much... I always dreamed that I could experience life like you... I have never drunk Coca-Cola..."

Zoe turned around. "Nick, do you have some Coke with you?"

Zoe put the can of Coke against the young woman's mouth, feeding her a tiny bit of the liquid.

"It's so sweet... I finally drank Coke..."

Zoe felt the woman's head falling on her chest. Her malnourished body was so thin it felt like no weight at all. Zoe turned to Nick. "What happened?"

Nick took the woman off Zoe and laid her body on the ground gently. "Zoe, she just passed away."

"Passed away?" It took Zoe a few seconds to understand Nick's words. She suddenly remembered something. "The baby. We need to help her baby."

Nick lifted Zoe to her feet. "The baby passed away a while ago. Let's go back to the car."

As their jeep drove on, Zoe observed the bodies scattered along the roadside in silence. Despite scientists warning the governments around the world for decades, no real actions had been taken to reduce greenhouse gas emissions, so it was no surprise that the global average temperature rose two degrees Celsius by 2026 compared with pre-industrial revolution temperatures. It was supposedly going to happen by the end of the twenty-first century. During the following decade, due to the soaring temperatures, weather patterns changed worldwide; crop harvests reduced dramatically, particularly in developing countries, and as a result, food shortages caused global famine. The mid-west of the US once again turned into a dust bowl. Food-exporting countries like the US and Australia only just produced enough food for their own people, so while the rich countries could still manage to feed their own people, the poor countries suffered great loss of life... While Zoe was lost in her own thoughts, she heard Nick suddenly say, "Why are we changing direction?"

Zoe then realized that their vehicle had peeled off from the main road. "Captain, that's not the direction to the airport."

"It's not, but we would never get to the airport in time if you insist on stopping to help collapsed mothers and crying babies," said the captain. "This way we'll have to drive a longer distance, but there will be far fewer people on the road, so we can drive much faster, and you will be able to catch your flight tonight."

The image that appeared on the wall was a UK passport. The 3D photo matched the young man standing in front of her. Olivia felt a great sense of relief. "Toby, your name is Toby."

"Toby. I suppose it's my name." There was no sign of any recognition from him.

"Nice to meet you, Toby." Olivia hugged him warmly. She was over the moon; after seeing his subdued reception, she calmed down a bit. An awkward silence fell between them briefly. She typed on her wrist, and the TV news appeared on her wall, on the northernmost tip of Australia, in front of the lined-up Australian warships, thousands of refugees' fishing boats covered the narrow sea between Australia and its neighbouring countries. A male voice reported, "After last night's storm, many boats sank, and an estimate of over a thousand people drowned. You are watching a report by Jonathan Media…"

"Why weren't these refugees allowed to get into Australia?" asked Toby.

Olivia found it very hard to answer Toby's very basic question. For decades, refugees had been an extremely sensitive topic in the Australian political landscape. In order to demonstrate their toughness toward people smugglers, politicians made some inhumane decisions to gain political points. As a result, those poor and vulnerable people were placed in indefinite detention, subject to unbearable living conditions. And that was well before the global warming-caused famine started… Just as she was struggling to find something to say, another breaking news story burst onto the screen. It took Olivia's breath away, literally.

It said that last night a group of religious extremists blew up the Australian AI laboratory. The explosion collapsed large parts of the building. Fortunately, there were very few employees inside the building at the time, but it had been confirmed that the chief scientist, Professor Smith, together with a couple of security guards, had been killed in the blast…

Olivia couldn't believe her ears. Tears flowed down her cheeks. She didn't hear the rest of the report. She just sat there and stared at the wall, eyes unfocused… Finally, Olivia was able to focus again, and she saw Toby was watching the news intently. How long had she lost focus? It couldn't have been too long, since the same piece of news was still being reported on the screen. Toby was completely immersed in the news, seemingly unaware of Olivia's reaction.

Then Toby turned to Olivia. "You seem quite upset by the news."

"Of course I am upset. People were killed."

"Who was Professor Smith? The name sounds very familiar," asked Toby.

"Didn't you hear? The news mentioned he was the chief scientist at the lab."

"Yes, I heard that, but the name means something to me; something far more than that. I wish I could remember what it is," Toby said.

Me too, Olivia thought to herself.

"What's your relationship with this man Professor Smith?" asked Toby.

"What makes you think there is a relationship between us?"

"I can tell from your body language," Toby said with confidence.

Olivia wiped her tears with the back of her hand and then said, "Professor Smith was Leo's father."

"Who's Leo?"

"Oh, I forgot to mention that Leo was my ex-boyfriend."

"I am so sorry."

Toby's voice and facial expression showed his genuine sorrow, and that made Olivia feel better. "John was a very good man, and one of the smartest scientists I've ever met."

"In my lost memories, I may know him very well." Toby shook his head. "Please tell me something about him. I mean Professor Smith."

"Professor Smith was one of the few scientists who truly believed that it is possible to create artificial consciousness. He has been working in the field for the last three decades..."

"Artificial consciousness?" Toby interrupted. "Do you mean artificial intelligent?"

"No, I mean artificial consciousness," said Olivia firmly.

"What's the difference?"

23

"Well, let me tell you a story first," said Olivia. "A guy is inside an enclosed room, and there are two slits in the wall; one opens to the inside, and the other to the outside. When a piece of paper is pushed through the in-slit, the guy's instructions are to find a shape-matching piece of paper from a pile of paper inside the room and then push it out through the out-slit. Despite the seemingly random squiggles on the paper that don't mean anything to him, by following the instructions, he performs his duty perfectly. The squiggles on the paper are in fact questions and answers written in Chinese, so from an outsider's viewpoint, this guy is proficient in the Chinese language and capable of understanding and answering questions in Chinese. It's called 'Chinese Room' in artificial consciousness terms."

"You mean artificial consciousness is about self-awareness?" asked Toby.

"You are getting there," nodded Olivia.

"Had he managed to create artificial consciousness?" Toby asked.

"Not that I know of." Olivia shook her head.

"You don't believe it's possible, do you?"

"What makes you say that?" asked Olivia curiously.

"I concluded it from your body language," Toby said simply.

"Well, I'll need to be more careful about my body language next time, especially in front of you." Olivia gazed at Toby, but there was no expression in his blue eyes.

"Body language can reveal one's most secret thoughts, and few people are able to hide it from skilful observers," said Toby in a matter-of-fact manner.

"It seems that you are such an expert in reading others' body language." Olivia paused. "And secret thoughts. What am I thinking now?"

"I don't need to decipher your body language this time; I can just read it from your face. You are wondering how and where I got such an ability. It could be a gift or I could be trained. All the answers are here but lost for the moment." Toby patted his own head. "Could I ask you a couple more questions?" Toby said carefully, and continued after Olivia nodded. "Why would someone want to blow up the lab?"

Olivia used a tissue to wipe her face, feeling a bit calmer. "Because these fanatics believe creating artificial consciousness is against God."

"Was there such an attack on the lab before?"

"A few report about threats and warnings but no real actions." Olivia got herself a glass of water, sipped a bit and then sat down on the sofa again.

"So the question is why they took action now. Could it be that Professor Smith had some kind of breakthrough recently?" asked Toby.

"Possibly," said Olivia thoughtfully. The news in the background became quite loud, so Olivia was about to turn it off but stopped. It was being reported that the police had found five people dead in an underground parking lot in central Sydney. The reporter said that, based on the initial investigation, the bodies belonged to the infamous international crime organization God's Wishes, so it could be an internal turf war.

"Definitely," Toby said, and his voice imitated the reporter's. It made Olivia laugh. She liked his sense of humour; it was so much like Leo's. However, what the reporter said next wiped out any light feeling from both of them.

"A confirmed source stated that the killing happened just after the explosion in the AI laboratory, so there is some speculation that there may be some connection between the two incidents..."

Toby exchanged a look with Olivia. "Are you thinking what I am thinking?"

"Maybe, but it's impossible..."

"I know exactly what's in your mind. Let's face it: I appeared in the underground parking lot just after the lab explosion. I had the skill to carry out the attack. I also seemingly have some connections to and knowledge about Professor Smith in my lost memories..."

"Yes, I did think along those lines." Olivia interrupted him. "But you risked your own life to save mine, so I don't believe you could be the one who carried out the attack."

"I could still be a fanatic," said Toby.

"You don't sound like one to me."

"How do you know that? That could be because I lost my memories."

"Hang on," Olivia said. "When you appeared in the parking lot to save my life, you hadn't lost your memories then. What you said and did didn't sound like a fanatic terrorist to me, and it definitely didn't sound like one who just blew up a whole lab."

"Thank you for trusting me, and I hope you are right."

"I know I am right; it's intuition. My intuition has been proved correct in the past." Olivia gazed into Toby's eyes. "You know I am telling the truth, don't you?"

Toby nodded and suddenly frowned. "You have a visitor, right outside of your door."

"Impossible." Olivia hadn't managed to complete a sentence when they heard a knock on the door.

4.   Global Warming

"How can we go back to headquarters without finding the Taibot bodyguard in question?" Nick asked quietly.

They were driving along a deserted road through the dry land. There was no grass, trees or any living plant in sight. The jeep stayed a reasonable distance away from the escorting military truck ahead in order to avoid its long, dusty tail. The captain was leaning his head against the headrest and had completely ignored Zoe during the last couple of hours of driving.

"Come on, Nick. We have been searching for the damn Taibot for over a month and can't carry on indefinitely," Zoe said in a low voice.

"Have we confirmed that it's not the Taibot who killed the tribe chief?"

"Of course we have." Zoe stared at Nick. "How could you ask such a question? You are a Taibot yourself. You know well that all Taibots manufactured in Australia have ethical codes imbedded in the chips in their heads. In this case, it's obvious the chief's brother killed him and blamed the Taibot."

"But without the Taibot, we can't prove the case."

"I don't think we'll ever find the Taibot. They could have completely destroyed it and made it disappear from the surface of the earth. I wish that every Taibot had a black box that could be located remotely; it'd make my job a lot easier. Why don't they have a bloody black box?"

"It's because of the privacy law..."

"Nick, that was a rhetorical question," Zoe said.

"Eh." Nick shook his head.

Olivia tapped her wrist once, and the visitor's image came up on her TV screen. It was her mother. Her mother must think she was sick since she hadn't answered her phone call.

Why did she always visit her at the most inconvenient moments?

"It's my mother. Toby, just tell her that we met yesterday on the street, and you need to stay with me for a few days."

Toby nodded.

While cursing internally, Olivia reluctantly opened the door and let her mother in.

As soon as she saw Toby, Olivia's mother's eyes brightened. "Oh, I didn't know you had a visitor. Hi, I am Liv's mother, Mia."

"Hi, Mia, nice to meet you. I am Toby."

"Nice to meet you too, Toby." Mia stared at Toby for a few seconds longer and then turned to Olivia. "Why haven't you mentioned Toby to me before?"

"It's because we only met yesterday," said Olivia. She tried very hard to think of an excuse to get rid of her mother.

"Oh, how lovely." Mia turned to Toby. "Toby, how did you two meet?"

Olivia spoke before Toby had a chance. "Mum, Toby and I have a few urgent things that need to be dealt with."

"All right." Mia laughed. "I am on my way to do some shopping in the city, so I will leave you alone." Mia walked toward the door but stopped. She turned to Toby. "Toby, we're having a family barbecue tomorrow afternoon. Would you be able to join us?"

How could she forget about the family gathering completely? Olivia was about to say that they had something already scheduled, but Toby said, "Thanks for your invitation, Mia. I am more than happy to attend as long as it's okay with Liv."

"Of course. Liv would like to introduce you to our family, so see you tomorrow then, Toby." Mia smiled broadly, walking out of the apartment.

"Why did you agree to attend my family's barbecue?" asked Olivia.

"I thought it'd be rude to decline such a lovely invitation."

"But I thought you didn't want to have anything to do with authorities." Olivia sat back on the sofa.

"It's hardly getting involved with authorities to attend your family gathering; besides, it'd cause more unnecessary attention if I didn't go."

Olivia thought about it and agreed that Toby's reasoning had some weight behind it. "If that's the case, you will need some clothes."

"There are quite a few in your wardrobe, and they seem to fit me perfectly."

"No, you can't wear them; they belonged to Leo," Olivia said firmly.

Toby nodded but didn't say anything.

Olivia tapped her wrist a few times. Racks and racks of clothes appeared on her TV screen. She flicked her fingers to zoom in on some racks. "What kind of clothes do you like?"

"Tomorrow is forecasted to be thirty-nine degrees, so a T-shirt and shorts would be suitable."

Olivia waved her hands, zooming and flapping through dozens more racks of clothes, but she failed to find anything that satisfied her. "Completely useless," she mumbled to herself, and then selected the customer design option. It didn't take long for Olivia to finish her own design.

"Take your clothes off." Olivia turned to Toby.

"What for?"

"You wear underwear, don't you? I just want to see if my design looks okay on you." Olivia felt amused at seeing Toby's reaction to her request.

Toby took off his clothes awkwardly and finally stood in front of Olivia in only his underwear.

Olivia observed Toby closely. Although not surprised, she was still amazed to see the perfect skin on his arms and legs; the gash wounds inflicted merely fifteen hours ago were completely gone. While admiring his perfect body, Olivia felt a heavy blanket of doubt falling onto her mind. She shook her head to get her focus back on what she was doing. She tapped a few more times on her wrist, and then her newly designed T-shirt and shorts appeared on Toby's body in a hologram form.

"What do you think?" Olivia gestured at the TV screen behind Toby.

Toby turned around, observing his own image on the wall for a while. "I like it; you should be a fashion designer."

That's exactly what Leo would say. Even the tone was exactly like Leo's as she remembered it. Why did she associate everything about Toby with Leo? She had to stop doing it. "The drone will be delivering the clothes to you shortly. You can put your clothes back on now."

Olivia then had an idea. "Toby, based on the delicious breakfast you made for me, it seems that you are quite good at cooking. I just wondered if you are also good at making dessert. Of course, you don't have to do it if you don't want to."

"I am more than happy to contribute to your family's gathering, and yes, I can make pavlova."

Olivia felt her heart skip a beat; this was just too much to be a coincidence. She tried to speak as normally as she could. "That'd be great. Everyone loves Pavlova. You would be the best guest ever in my family's history."

"You seem very excited about the idea of me making Pavlova, but the reason is not what you said."

Olivia smiled. "So you confess that you can't work out what I am thinking."

Toby shook his head. "Women's minds are the hardest thing to understand in the whole universe."

Olivia dreamed about Toby, and suddenly Leo walked into the apartment. Toby and Leo started having an argument; Leo pointed a gun at Toby and was about to shoot him. "Oh, no," Olivia cried out loud.

"Are you all right?" Toby asked from outside of her bedroom door.

It took a second for Olivia to work out what had happened. "I am okay; just a nightmare."

"I have nightmares, too. Good night."

"Thanks, Toby. Good night." Olivia smiled to herself.

"What time are we supposed to be there?" asked Toby. It was late morning the next day, Sunday.

Olivia looked at her wrist. "Two-ish, I guess."

"In that case, we need to get the ball rolling." Toby opened the fridge. "We don't have any eggs."

"Of course you don't have eggs," said the fridge. "It's because eggs are rationed and every person is only allowed an egg every fortnight."

"Really?" Toby turned to Olivia.

"Toby, don't you know about the food ration?"

Toby shook his head. "It might be part of my lost memories. Please explain it to me."

"There's not much to explain. Due to global warming, harvests dropped significantly around the world, and Australia is struggling to produce enough grain for its own people, so there is no extra to feed domestic animals. As a result, meat, milk, eggs, and any other animal-related food products are strictly rationed."

"What about agricultural technologies? Can't we produce some kind of new crops that are able to grow in hotter climates? Or in controlled environments indoors?"

Olivia shook her head. "I don't fully understand the science, but it seems there is no such crop being produced. There are many large parking lot-like buildings used to grow vegetables. They are called vertical farms, but they are insufficient to supply the whole population."

"Close my door to save energy; don't you know about global warming?" shouted the fridge.

"Oh, sorry." Toby closed the fridge's door. "I thought it was called climate change back in 2018," said Toby.

So he was able to remember things back then; that was eighteen years ago. Based on Toby's passport, he was only eighteen in 2018. Olivia wondered if Toby could remember anything else from that period. Well, that was eight years before she met Leo for the first time, and she was only ten years old then. "It's still called climate change now; I just used to call it global warming. Climate change would be more accurate because weather becomes much colder in some regions."

Toby nodded. "I remember reading about that; although most people believed in climate change, not many believed it would happen so soon. Everyone thought it'd get a bit warmer and the sea level would rise a few inches by the end of the century. That's even what it said in the IPCC's report, so how could it change so dramatically in such a short time?"

"You don't remember anything about what happened in the last eighteen years, do you?" Olivia continued after Toby shook his head. "IPCC underestimated climate change completely. The climate change models used in the study assumed linear progress of global weather and ecosystems, but in reality, the situation has been deteriorating exponentially due to many self-reinforcement loops near the Arctic Circle."

"Self-reinforcement loops?" asked Toby.

"After the ice in the Arctic Circle shrank due to the higher temperatures caused by climate change, the darker ocean water absorbed more sunlight, rather than the white ice surface reflecting it. That resulted in even bigger temperature rises, which caused more ice to melt, and so on. It's a downward death-spiral..."

"I see..." Toby stared at her in disbelief.

32

Olivia laughed bitterly. "Just recently the average global temperature has reached three degrees warmer than pre-industrial levels. Bushfires destroyed most of the Amazon rainforest last year, and global food production plummeted."

"Oh dear, there must be a global famine now," Toby murmured.

"You can say that again." Olivia sighed. "Over two hundred million people died last year due to food shortage, disease, and civil wars around the world. Scientists estimate that if the crop harvest conditions are not improved next year, millions, even billions, will perish…"

"My God, I would never have imagined that it could become so bad," said Toby. He thought about it and then said, "I assume most of those deaths occurred in poor countries?"

"Yes, of course; Africa, South America, Asia, the Pacific, and the Middle East. Poor people have paid with their lives for westerners' accumulation of wealth." Olivia wiped away her tears.

"What happened to the rich countries? I mean Europe and the US," asked Toby.

Before Olivia spoke again, the fridge said, "Well, southern Europeans migrated to Scandinavian regions, and the US merged with Canada, becoming United Canada, or UC. Apparently all Canadians voted 'overwhelmingly and willingly to merge with the US.'"

Toby turned to the fridge. "Very impressive. You are such a politically savvy fridge, aren't you?"

"Well, this is all on the Internet; all you need to do is look. I have a lot of free time, so I read quite a bit," said the fridge. "Here are just a few such examples."

Toby stared at the fast-rolling articles and images on the TV screen on the fridge's front door and then shouted, "Stop! Back a bit. Yes, that article about the methane threat in the Arctic region."

He read the article with rapt interest.

The release of the potent greenhouse gas from the Arctic Ocean floor does not only increase the global temperature; unlike CO_2, methane is flammable. Even in air-methane concentrations as low as five percent, the mixture could ignite from lightning or some other spark and send fireballs tearing across the sky. The effect would be much like the "vacuum bombs" used by the US and Russian armies, igniting fuel droplets above a target: those near the ignition point are obliterated instantly, and those at the fringes are likely to suffer many internal injuries, including burst eardrums, severe concussion, ruptured lungs and internal organs, and possibly blindness...

"I am glad that you noticed it too," said the fridge. "Methane released from the permanently frozen soil and seabed in the Arctic could terminate all complex forms of life on Earth instantly..."

"Really?" Toby turned to Olivia. "Do you know much about the methane threat?"

Olivia shook her head. "Not much, and I don't want to know about it either. I suggest that we should keep the ball rolling."

Toby nodded.

"Fridge, order a dozen eggs, and use express delivery," Olivia said.

"My lady, that'd be half your yearly allowance," said the fridge.

"Shut up and follow the order," Olivia said.

"I was just politely reminding you about your food supply situation; it's my duty as your food keeper... All right, I'll carry out your command right now," said the fridge.

Olivia watched Toby preparing to make Pavlova with great interest. His every move, gesture and expression was just too much like Leo's to be coincidence.

"To cook the perfect Pavlova, I would suggest setting the temperature and timer as displayed. That is my recommendation, by the way," said the oven.

Olivia tapped her wrist a few times to disable the oven's speech function, and then turned to Toby. "They are really annoying sometimes."

"Whoever programmed it must have a sense of humour." Toby put the Pavlova into the oven.

"I don't think any human programmed them. I believe that all programs are made by other programs now." Olivia watched Toby closely, but there was no sign of anything in his expression.

"Oh, I probably would have known that if I hadn't lost my memories." Toby paused, thinking for a few seconds. "While I was making the Pavlova, I had this strange feeling, like I could suddenly remember something, but because it was only a piece or a hint, I was unable to link it to any memories. It's so frustrating."

"Just relax; you'll recover your memories soon." Olivia patted his arm.

"I hope so. Thanks," said Toby, smiling.

She liked his smile. Of course, it was just like Leo's. Olivia was completely confused; had she lost her mind?

Olivia opened the door and walked onto her balcony. Toby, who held the Pavlova, followed. A flying car zoomed in, hovering next to the balcony. Olivia pushed open the gate that was part of the balcony handrail and stepped into the car.

"Oceanside picnic site 27," Olivia said after Toby had climbed in beside her. "Please stay with me and let me do all the talking."

Toby nodded.

Apart from the narrow strip between Sydney and Melbourne that was still inhabitable, much of the Australian continent had become desert. Large chunks of the Australian population had squeezed into Tasmania Island. They were flying to one of the few special designated picnic spots that were not suitable for growing crops. Olivia watched the landscape underneath their flying car. "I can't believe Australia was once a food exporting country."

"It seems that you are at least producing enough food for your own people," said Toby.

"It's lucky we don't have a large population. Thinking about it, Australia is as guilty as the rest of the large greenhouse gas emitters because we extracted coal and gas out of the ground and sold them to fuel global warming," said Olivia. "Human beings are supposedly more intelligent, but we still dug our own graves, driven by greed."

"Do you think humans will survive this time?" asked Toby.

"Millions and millions of people are dying around the globe as temperatures are getting hotter and less food is being produced, so I very much doubt it," said Olivia. "I never imagined that I'd live to see the end of humanity."

"How much time do you think is left for humans on Earth?"

Olivia leaned back against her seat and closed her eyes for a moment. "Someone predicted a couple of decades, but someone said only a few years; nobody really knows. One thing is clear: human extinction is just a matter of time. After eradicating most other life forms from the surface of the earth, can humans survive alone?"

They spent the rest of the journey in silence. Finally, they arrived.

"My lady, would you like me to wait for you here?" asked the instrument panel.

"Would it be cheaper for you to wait here?" asked Olivia.

"It depends on how long I have to wait. If you'll be back within a couple of hours, it'd be much cheaper for me to wait here."

Olivia looked at Toby and then said, "It'll definitely be within two hours, I'll make sure of it."

"Okay, have a nice time, and I'll be ready to take you back home in two hours' time." The car flew away after they stepped out of it.

"Hello, Toby. It's so nice to see you again." Olivia's mother Mia hugged Toby. "Let me introduce you…"

"Mum, I'll do the introductions," Olivia said. "Toby, this is Cooper, my father; Zara, my mother's sister; Max, Zara's husband; and Grace and Jack, my cousins."

After Toby said hello and shook hands with everyone, Olivia said, "Toby is from the UK and in the middle of backpacking across the world. We met a couple of days ago. He will stay with me for a few days before figuring out his next move."

"How lovely. Toby, do you have brothers or sisters?" asked Zara.

"I can't remember," said Toby.

5. Picnic

Olivia watched people's confused expressions and quickly said, "Toby means that he has been travelling for so long that he can't even remember about his own family. Toby has a very dry sense of humour."

"Pretty dry, indeed." Toby made a funny face and everyone laughed.

"Toby, half of Holland is underwater, and the European Union has been moving people from the Mediterranean to Scandinavia since last summer. What is the situation in your hometown in the UK?" asked Max.

Olivia felt very tense while waiting for Toby's reply.

"Well, I only know what's reported on the news, so you know as much as I do," said Toby casually.

Olivia felt great relief. During the following conversations, she was glad that Toby adapted to the situation extremely well. He hadn't made a second mistake to reveal the fact that he had no memories of current events. She was impressed by Toby's quick thinking and great wits. In a few scenarios, she couldn't think of a better response.

"Zara, are you aware of the methane threat from the Arctic regions?" Toby asked after discussing and answering tons of questions about his family in the UK.

Zara looked at her sister, then Olivia, and finally said, "I am always so busy, so I never have time to read the news."

Mia nodded in agreement. She turned to Olivia's father. "Cooper, I think we should get the barbecue started, don't you think?"

Toby took a big drag of his beer and then said, "Max, how long do you think humanity will last?"

Olivia noticed Grace was sitting away from the crowd, alone. She knew Grace had been struggling with bad depression for a while, and she was quite sure this kind of dystopia conversation wouldn't do her mental condition any good.

Max threw his empty beer bottle to the ground and opened another one. "A few decades, maybe longer; who knows? Mate, I don't know about humanity, but I'm pretty sure Aussies will be the last ones standing on Earth."

"How can you be so sure?" asked Toby.

"Toby, do you know why people say Australia is a lucky country? I'll tell you why: we are a bunch of lucky people, so we will be the last to go…"

Olivia grabbed Toby's hand before he managed to say anything else. "Toby, let's go and help Dad with the cooking."

Toby stood by the barbecue while Olivia's father grilled the meat. "Cooper, I thought meat was extremely rare and rationed, so how do you have so much?"

"Cooper and I kept a pig in our backyard, so it's possible to have a family treat like this," said Mia.

"Where do you get food to feed the pig?" asked Toby.

"We collect all the food scraps from friends' places. It's more like a community project. Of course, in the end, everyone can have a share of the meat." Mia spoke proudly.

"It seems you guys still have plenty of food to eat, so why would the government introduce food rationing?" asked Toby.

Before Mia could come up with the words, Olivia spoke first. "Well, Australia used to be a food exporter, so even with the crop harvest reduction, it still produces sufficient food to sustain its own population. I suppose that food rationing is to reduce food waste, and also for humanitarian and strategic reserve purposes."

Silence fell. Nobody spoke for a while, and then Toby said, "Cooper, it seems that humans are unlikely to survive global warming; is there anything anyone can do to get us through this crisis?"

"Wu Wei is the best way to act," said Cooper.

Looking at Toby's face, Olivia laughed. "Toby, my father is the oriental philosophy professor at the Australian National University. He specializes in Taoism, so his words can be very hard to understand sometimes."

"I'll leave you to your philosophical discussions." Mia rolled her eyes and walked away to join the others.

"Taoism? Wu Wei?" Toby thought for a second. "The Way that can be told of is not an eternal way..."

"The names that can be named are not eternal names..." Cooper patted Toby's back, and they both laughed.

"Cooper, based on my recent research, the concept of Wu Wei is very difficult to grasp. The interpretations of it include inaction, respecting nature, not interfering with nature, etc., but none of them are satisfactory to me," said Toby.

Cooper nodded. "Wu Wei is the fundamental principle of Taoism and not an explicit concept, so it's no surprise that there have been so many different interpretations over the last two thousand years..."

Olivia knew that they were talking about Taoism, an ancient philosophy originating from China over two and a half thousand years ago. While Toby and Cooper exchanged their understandings of Taoism, Olivia felt both excited and disappointed. She was excited because it seemed as if Toby had recovered some of his memories about Taoism; her disappointment was because Leo and she had never understood the incomprehensible words that had occupied her father's whole career. This fact had profound implications on her current situation.

Olivia stood there and listened to their conversations patiently, although her brain didn't take in one word. Finally she heard Toby say hesitantly, "Cooper, would you like me to help you grill the meat?"

"That'd be great. Here you go. I'll go and sit down for a cold drink." Cooper walked away.

"Liv, I have a strange feeling that I have been here before," Toby said quietly.

"That's good; it means that your memories are starting to come back," said Olivia.

Toby looked around and then thought for a while. "All of these surroundings look so familiar; I feel like I've been here before. It's so strange."

"There is nothing strange about it; this is a popular picnic spot, and you could have been here before."

Toby looked at Olivia's family again and said in a low voice, "Not only this picnic spot, but also with your family, grilling on this barbecue, with you standing beside me..."

This shocked Olivia. She didn't know what to say. Before she could respond, Jack came over. He was a seventeen-year-old high school student. "Hi, Toby, your hair looks awesome. Can I touch it?"

"No," Olivia said before Toby could open his mouth.

"Be cool, man." Jack walked away.

"Why did you say no? He just wanted to touch my hair," asked Toby.

"I'll explain it to you later. It seems that the meat is done. Let's eat and leave as soon as possible."

Everyone loved Toby's Pavlova. Toby could tell that they meant it and were not just being polite. But he could also tell when they lied to him. For example, when Olivia said he was a backpacker from the UK, although everyone nodded and smiled, he knew nobody believed it. Toby knew he had been here before, with Olivia and her family, but how could it be possible? He didn't know Olivia at all; seeing her in the underground parking lot was his first memory of her.

Fortunately he didn't have to wonder for very long because Olivia told everyone that they had to leave due to an urgent appointment. After their flying car took off from the ground, Toby said, "Please explain why everyone is lying to me."

Olivia stared at the instrument panel in front of them and said, "Not here; wait until we get home first."

Zoe heard the sound of explosions. Lifting her eyes, she saw plumes of smoke beside and behind them. Their jeep jolted to a sudden stop. The command device on the captain's hand shouted loudly in the local language of the soldiers on the truck in front of them. Nick translated.

"Captain, we are under attack...they don't want to shoot us, they just want us to stop..."

Even before the captain could reply, a different voice sounded from his command device in English. "Captain, this is Commander Congo, and I trust you have heard about me."

The captain turned around, glancing at Zoe and Nick.

"Commander Congo is a rebel leader and infamous for his cannibalism," said Nick in a low voice.

"I heard that. Yes, I am the famous Commander Congo who eats people's flesh. It's not a bad solution when not much food is available in this part of the world; well, it's not very good for those people being eaten, but at least my guys can survive." After a loud shout of laughter, the voice spoke again. "Captain, it's your lucky day. Normally I would kill you and all of your soldiers to feed my followers, but I'll let you go if you leave the white guy, the white girl, and the jeep to me. I've always wanted to eat a white woman, so today is my lucky day. What do you say?"

The captain glanced at Zoe once more and said, "How can I be sure that you will let my soldiers and me leave safely?"

"You can go in the truck and leave the white guy and girl inside the jeep behind. Don't do anything stupid; otherwise you will be destroyed instantly. The reason you haven't been killed yet is because I want both the white girl and the jeep unspoiled."

"I need time to consider your offer," said the captain.

"I give you five minutes; if you don't do as I say, your truck will be blown up first. Your time starts now." The voice cut out.

The captain turned off his command device. "You heard our conversation then. It seems that we don't have much choice."

"Why did you choose this route in the first place?" asked Zoe, while watching the captain closely.

"I swear that Commander Congo has never been around this region before," said the captain.

"It's true," said Nick.

Zoe thought for a moment. "As you just said, it seems that we don't have much choice now, so why don't you and your soldiers leave here and let them have me and the jeep?"

"I can't do that, my lady."

"Why not? As you said earlier, you would have killed me yourself, so now is the perfect opportunity, and you don't even have to do it."

"It's true that we all hate your westerners for what you have done to destroy our home and kill our people, but as a solider, it's my duty to protect you and escort you safely to the airport. I'll do just that, even if it means I lose my life," said the captain.

"I thank you for your bravery, but it seems there is not much chance for us to fight back," said Zoe.

"What should I do then?" asked the captain.

"Leave. You and your soldiers leave and let them have Zoe and me," said Nick.

6. Taibots

As soon as they entered Olivia's apartment, Toby asked, "Please tell me why everyone was lying to me, and why Jack wanted to touch my hair and you said no to him."

Olivia didn't answer immediately. She got herself a glass of water, sitting down on the sofa.

"So?" Toby pressed.

After sipping a bit of water, Olivia said, "Do you know anything about Taibot?"

"Taibot? I don't think so. What is it?"

She nodded. "It must be part of your lost memories again. After True Artificial Intelligence was born in 2026, programs were no longer written by humans but by other programs, like I mentioned earlier; since then, innovations have been growing exponentially."

"If that's the case, how come True Artificial Intelligence couldn't help to solve the global warming problems?"

Olivia drank a mouthful of water. "Although scientific societies kept warning the governments and public consistently, no drastic measures were taken to address global warming until 2025, but it was already too late then. Earth has passed the point of no return, and dozens of CO_2 self-reinforcing feedback loops started... No science or technology would be able to save human beings and other living species from extinction due to the downward death spiral of global temperatures rising..."

Toby thought for a while but said nothing.

Olivia shook her head, refocusing on the topic, and then continued. "With the help of the True Artificial Intelligence, we soon solved the energy storage problem. As a result, we were able to completely switch to renewable energy, but of course it's far too late."

She saw no reaction from Toby, so she continued. "The next breakthrough with nanotechnology and bio-computing brought us the True Artificial Intelligence Bot, or Taibot, as we call them."

"How intelligent are these Taibots?"

"Well, that depends on your definition of intelligence," said Olivia. "If you mean reasoning, deducting, memorizing, and researching, they are far superior to humans, but they don't have consciousness; in other words, all of their decisions are made based on the databases in their brains."

"Can one tell the difference between a Taibot and a real human easily?"

Olivia chose her words carefully. "Of course, Taibots have very low emotional intelligence."

Toby thought for a while and said, "What do Taibots have to do with my original questions?"

Olivia didn't speak, just stared at Toby.

Toby then suddenly shouted out, "Oh no, don't tell me all of your relatives thought I was a Taibot. But why?"

"Because of your perfect body; because it's unheard of to meet a real human guy on the street who wants to attend my family's gathering. Because...would you like me to continue?"

"What do you think? Do you think I am a Taibot?"

"I did have my doubts from time to time, but I don't think you are a Taibot."

"What were your doubts about me?"

Olivia collected her thoughts and then said carefully, "First was how quickly you recovered from your wounds; no human is capable of that. Your body is too perfect for a real human."

"Okay, why do you think I am not a Taibot then?"

"As I mentioned before, you have emotional intelligence; more accurately, you have real human consciousness."

Toby laughed. "There is no convincing evidence to form that conclusion. I could be the latest model of Taibot who has real human consciousness."

Olivia stood and walked up to Toby, standing very close. She gazed into Toby's eyes, only a couple of inches away.

"Taibots do not have human consciousness, and I can see your soul in your eyes. That's enough evidence to convince me you are a real human. If you really want to know, it's intuition that Taibots are not capable of having."

"Intuition? Do you mean making decisions without thinking?"

"Yes, exactly." Olivia never moved her gaze away from Toby's eyes.

"I suppose that I have done it sometimes. For instance, I made up my mind to save you in the underground parking lot without thinking whether I was capable of fighting off the thugs."

Olivia smiled broadly. "You see; this proves that you have real human consciousness."

Toby thought for a second. "Why did Jack want to touch my hair?"

"Because he wanted to check if you have an implanted receiver behind your ear." Olivia sat back down on the sofa again.

"What's a receiver?" Toby fumbled behind his ears.

"You don't have one," Olivia said. "I checked you myself while you were sleeping. Sorry for the suspicion."

"Do all Taibots have these receivers?"

"As far as I know," said Olivia.

"Surely I can do a brain scan to prove if I am a Taibot or not."

Olivia shook her head. "It's not that simple; because of the nanotechnology and bio-computing, a scan would reveal nothing. Besides, some humans have implanted chips to enhance their strength, speed, and abilities, to access the Internet, etc. In other words, a scan wouldn't be able to tell the difference between a Taibot and a human with implanted chips."

"There must be some way to find out if I am a Taibot or not," said Toby in frustration.

"Yes, there is; through surgery and the use of special equipment to check the chips in your brain." Olivia took a deep breath. "I have encountered many smart Taibots due to my connections with Leo, so I know something about Taibots. Based on my experience and observations, you are not a Taibot."

Toby walked to the window, looking out. "How do you explain my body and my impossible healing ability?"

"You could be one of the genetic engineering experiments, who knows?" Olivia said. "It seems that some of your memories are starting to come back, at least the part about Taoism. Can you remember anything else?"

Nick signalled the captain to make sure the command device was turned off. "Based on my research on Commander Congo, and on the firepower he just demonstrated, he was not bluffing; he could easily take all of us out right now, so it's meaningless trying to fight back. We are inside his ambush and just have to do as he asked. We have no choice."

"It's my duty to protect you; I can't just give up on you," said the captain.

Nick raised his hand to stop the conversation. "We don't have a lot of time to argue right now; otherwise, we'll all die here. Captain, take your soldiers and leave."

The captain thought for a moment. "To do my duty as a solider, I have made my decision to die with you." He then switched on the command device and gave the order for his soldiers to leave. "Commander Congo, I trust that you heard my order to my soldiers. Please keep your word and let them leave. I'll stay with these two white fellows and die, as is my duty."

"Captain, I admire your bravery and your sense of honour and duty. There aren't many real soldiers like you left nowadays. I promise that my men won't eat you after you are killed. I'll allow you to be buried as a soldier."

After the escorting truck with all the soldiers departed, Olivia saw blobs of dust approaching them from all directions, soon materializing as dozens of four-wheel drives, off road-type vehicles full of armed men. The truck-mounted guns must have fired the warning shots earlier. It didn't take long for a wall of armed men to surround Zoe's jeep.

A tall black guy pushed the human wall apart. "Welcome to Commander Congo's reception party." He laughed loudly at his own joke.

Commander Congo looked at least six foot seven, with broad shoulders and a huge chest and arm muscles. The warrior markings on his face made him scary under the scorching sunlight. Zoe wasn't a girl who could be intimidated easily, but upon seeing his sharp white teeth in his wide-open mouth, she couldn't help but shudder. She felt a spasm of cold run down her spine. She didn't want to imagine that the beast-like mouth would soon engulf her flesh.

"Open the door for our noble guests." Commander Congo turned, grinning at his followers.

One man put his AK47 on his shoulder and opened the jeep's door for Zoe.

Zoe's knees were too weak to walk. Fortunately Nick caught her before she collapsed to the ground. From the corner of her eye, she sensed the captain also standing beside her, but she didn't turn her head to look.

"Look what we've got here: two well-fed white meatloaves." Commander Congo turned to his men, who laughed loudly at his comment.

Zoe heard Nick's voice. "We understand that you are going to eat us, so I plead with you to kill us humanely."

Commander Congo stared at Nick for a moment, as if he had just discovered Nick's existence. "Big white guy, I'll eat you first and keep the white lady a little longer. White meats are hard to get nowadays." A round of loud laughter followed.

Zoe sensed Nick's arms, still around her, were getting tense, and then she heard Nick speak again. "Commander Congo, I heard that you have absolute loyalty from your followers; they treat you like their God."

"You are not wrong." Commander Congo scanned the armed men around him, speaking proudly.

As Zoe tried to work out what Nick was doing, she felt her body being thrown at the captain violently; at the same time, she saw Nick's body shoot at Commander Congo like an arrow. Moving in a blurred shadow, Nick's arm locked around Commander Congo's neck while his other hand held a gun against Commander Congo's chest. It seemed that the gun belonged to Commander Congo. The whole process happened so quickly. Before anyone could understand what was going on, Commander Congo became Nick's hostage.

"Commander Congo, let's test the loyalty of your followers." Nick turned to the armed men. "You have seen how fast I can be, so please don't try to shoot me, because I'll make sure to kill your commander before I die."

"Put all of your guns down. Now!" shouted Commander Congo.

To his credit, the armed men all lowered their guns. "White guy, what do you want to do now? You know you'll never get out of here today," said Commander Congo.

"We can discuss it later," said Nick. "Let the lady and the captain leave with the jeep, and I'll stay."

"What are you saying, Nick?" shouted the captain. "Take him with us, and we can all leave together."

"Yes, Nick, come with us," said Zoe with renewed courage.

"No, you both go, now," said Nick firmly. "Tell me when you are in a safe zone. Commander Congo and I will stay here and wait for your phone call."

7. Sunday Night

Olivia stared at Toby, waiting for his response and hoping that he had remembered something else, but his strange expression alarmed her.

"You have a visitor," said Toby.

This was the second time Toby had sensed someone was outside of her door. He might have super hearing, smelling, or some other sixth sense abilities similar to his impossible self-healing. Olivia didn't show any surprise or ask questions; she just turned to look at the monitor screen. Sure enough, a person appeared under her camera lens.

After the person pushed the doorbell and lifted her face to the camera, Olivia couldn't believe her eyes; it was Zoe. How could this be? Zoe was supposed to be coming home late tonight. Olivia glanced back at Toby quickly and then opened the door.

"Zoe, what a surprise! I thought you'd be back late tonight." Olivia hugged Zoe warmly, but she soon realized that something was not quite right; Zoe looked exhausted.

"Yeah, caught an early flight," said Zoe. She then turned, looking at Toby. "You are?"

Zoe was five foot nine, with dark hair and a very athletic body. She had a hint of an American accent. Just as Toby began to say something, Olivia interrupted. "Oh, let me introduce you to each other. Zoe, this is Toby, and Toby, this is Zoe, my roommate I told you about," said Olivia.

"Nice to meet you." Toby shook Zoe's hand, but Zoe turned, looking at Olivia with a large question mark on her face.

"Toby is backpacking here and needs a place to stay; since you were not here, I let him crash for a few days."

"Is that so?" Zoe gazed at Toby's eyes, observing him intensely.

50

"Yes. I really appreciate Olivia's and your hospitality in allowing me to stay," said Toby.

"Liv, how did you guys meet?" Zoe's gaze was still on Toby's face.

"Well, we bumped into each other on the street, literally, and started talking. Toby mentioned that he was looking for accommodation, so I let him stay with me for a while until he is able to find somewhere else."

"Wow, a fairy tale encounter," said Zoe. Her voice had no "wow" at all. She kept her gaze steadily on Toby's face.

"Oh no, we are just friends," said Toby quickly.

"Just friends?" Zoe turned back to Olivia.

"There is no fairy tale in the real world. We are just friends," said Olivia calmly. "Zoe, you look exhausted. Can I get something for you? A drink of some description?"

Zoe shook her head. "I am exhausted, and also starving. Liv, would you like to accompany me to go out and get something to eat?" Zoe then turned to Toby. "I hope you don't mind."

"Of course not," said Toby casually.

It wasn't very late, so there were still lots of people wandering on the street. Zoe sat down at a window table opposite Olivia in their favourite sushi restaurant.

"Ladies, could I have your ration coupons please?" said the waiter.

"We are not going to have any food, just a couple of drinks," said Zoe impatiently.

"Coupons may still be required, because some drinks are made from food. What would you like to have?" asked the waiter.

After they had settled down and the waiter had left, Zoe looked at Olivia. "Tell me the truth. Who is this guy Toby?"

Olivia hesitated, and then made up her mind. "Why are you suspicious of Toby?"

Zoe turned, looking through the window glass. "Come on, Liv. When's the last time you heard about a girl meeting a real human guy on the street who not only had a perfect body but was also happy to remain just friends with her?" Zoe didn't turn her head around while speaking.

"So you suspect Toby is not human?"

Zoe turned around, staring at Olivia. "Don't tell me the question never crossed your mind."

Olivia sipped her drink. "Of course it did, but I decided that he is not a Taibot, because no Taibot could present emotional intelligence as Toby does. I mean that he has real human consciousness." Olivia expected counter-arguments from Zoe to challenge her conclusions, but Zoe fell into silence. Quite unusual indeed. Olivia didn't push, just sitting there and waiting for Zoe's reply.

Zoe took a large gulp of her drink, then finally said, "Did you fall for him?"

Olivia thought for a second. "Not sure, but I am warming up toward him, I suppose."

Zoe took one more gulp and then shook her head and laughed bitterly. "Fuck it. If you like him, go for it; it doesn't matter if he is human or not."

"What's the matter, Zoe?"

Zoe turned her head toward the window, using a tissue to wipe her tears. She finally looked at Olivia again. "I lost...Nick...he sacrificed himself to save my life..."

"Nick? Isn't he your Taibot partner?"

"He was."

Olivia chose her words carefully. "I thought the relationship between you two was purely professional..."

"A bit more than that. Actually lots more than that," interrupted Zoe.

"I thought he was just a Taibot, with no real consciousness..." Olivia didn't know if she had said the right thing.

52

"I know." Zoe blew her nose with a handful of tissues. "I never regarded Nick as more than a tool until I lost him. It's amazing for me to discover I actually loved him, and I still do."

"I am so sorry..."

"In terms of your comments that Taibots don't have real consciousness," said Zoe, "I am not so sure about it now. Nick definitely had consciousness." Zoe put her hand over her forehead, speaking slowly. "Nick may not have had the same consciousness as a human, but he definitely had his own consciousness in his own right. There may be many different kinds of consciousness; you know, a Taibot consciousness."

Olivia thought about the concept for a moment. "You could have a point there. I have never thought about consciousness in that way. Think about it: we have only experienced human consciousness and are unable to imagine there could be other types of consciousness."

"Exactly." Zoe spoke with renewed energy in her voice. "It's just like a person would never dream about an elephant if he doesn't know that elephants exist."

"I wish Leo was here so he could explain the concept of consciousness more clearly." Olivia leaned back against her seat. "Anyway, based on my superficial understanding about consciousness, the difference between humans and Taibots is that Taibots lack self-consciousness. In other words, they just follow some sets of rules, regardless of how sophisticated or complex these rules are, and are not aware of their own existence."

Zoe blew her nose once more. "I knew that Nick was programmed to protect me, to follow my orders, and to assist me with his super-fast and clever brain...but you know, he was so considerate, tender, and able to make great conversation..."

"I wish that I had a chance to know him." Again, Olivia wasn't sure it was the right thing to say.

"Yeah, it's a pity you two never met. I am sure that you would like Nick; how could anyone not like him?" Zoe's voice faded slowly.

A long silence fell between them.

Finally Olivia decided to cheer Zoe up a bit. "When I talked to Sophie and Ava last week, we discussed going to the coast and having a weekend retreat together next week." Olivia didn't mention that Ava wanted to bring her new Taibot boyfriend, Luke, with them.

Zoe sipped her drink, staring at an invisible point behind Olivia's left shoulder for a while. She then said with a hollow voice, "Yeah that sounds great. When's the last time we had a vacation together?"

"Must be just after our graduation from college." Olivia pretended she was trying to remember the exact date, but it was purely for Zoe's benefit. She would never forget that date: it was the day Leo died.

It seemed that Zoe soon realized this very fact. She focused on Olivia's face. "Thank you for putting up with me. I'd like to have a vacation with you guys; it'd be good for me."

"Great," Olivia said. "I'll let Sophie and Ava know. I am sure that Ava will immediately jump on the chance and make all the bookings. You must be exhausted. Let's go back home and you can have a good rest."

Zoe nodded. "I'll stay with my mother for a few days; I need to see her anyway." She picked up her handbag, standing up. While they stood on the street waiting for their taxi, Zoe hugged Olivia. "Toby seems like a decent guy. Based on my brief observations, I agree with you that it is unlikely he is a Taibot. If he were, he would be the latest model nobody has ever heard about. Anyway, go for it if you like him."

"Thanks, Zoe." Olivia hugged Zoe tightly.

8. Monday

Zoe was woken by the Ixis on her wrist. Glancing at the display through half-closed eyes, she realized that it was her boss, Harry. Why was he ringing her while she was on her much-deserved leave? Didn't he realize that she had spent several hard and horrible months on her mission and also lost her partner? Couldn't it wait until she went back to work next week? She had been through the debriefing in Europe before flying back to Sydney, so it had to be something else. While cursing internally, Zoe reluctantly tapped her wrist to answer the phone call. Of course, she didn't enable the video-conference function.

"Hi, Harry, what's up?"

"Sorry to interrupt your vacation, but very unfortunately, we need you to come to the office today."

"What's it about?"

"I can't talk about it on the phone. Are you able to come to my office, now?"

Zoe had to make a great effort not to swear at her boss. Finally she said flatly, "I'll try my best to get to your office as soon as I can."

"Zoe, I appreciate it; see you soon."

"Toby, why don't you use the dishwasher?" Olivia picked up her handbag, ready to leave for work.

"It's only a couple of dishes. I don't mind doing it," said Toby while drying the plates.

It made Olivia smile; Leo used to say the same line. She found Toby more and more like Leo in his way of speaking and doing things, even how he walked. Although she knew that Toby wasn't Leo, Olivia liked the resemblance between the two; it made her like Toby more. She didn't know how to put it more clearly, but she liked Toby in his own way, but those ways were also similar to Leo.

"Do what you like. What are you going to do today?"

"Not quite sure yet. I'll have a look at the Internet. Maybe I'll find something to trigger my memories," said Toby.

"All right. Please stay inside; remember, someone out there may want to harm you, and you have no idea who they might be."

"I know that. It seems that your taxi has arrived. Have a nice day."

Olivia opened the glass sliding door, walking onto her balcony. Sure enough, a taxi was hovering and waiting for her. She wished she could have Toby's ability to sense objects without visual assistance; it could be handy sometimes, she thought as she stepped into the taxi.

"State public library," said Olivia to the instrument panel in front of her.

Zoe walked into Harry's office. She tried to behave as nicely as possible while staring at his bald head. "Hi, Harry, good morning."

Harry was in his mid-sixties. He quickly stood up from behind his desk, walking to Zoe and shaking her hand. "Welcome back, Zoe."

"Harry, what's all this about?"

Harry gestured Zoe to sit in the guest chair in front of his desk. "Anything to drink?"

Zoe shook her head.

"I have to use my ration card to get this damn cup of coffee, can you believe it?" Harry went back and sat in his chair behind his large desk.

"There isn't enough food to go around, and there are even fewer coffee beans. Do you know how many people have died from starvation in Africa this year alone? So you shouldn't complain too much."

Harry sighed. "I know. When I was young, you could eat as many hamburgers as you liked." He patted his abdomen. "I haven't had any meat for ages. Well, it's not all bad news. At least I have a smaller belly as a result of the food rationing."

Zoe had to agree with him; the global food shortage had reduced the waistlines in Australia significantly.

"Harry, what's this secret you can't talk about on the phone?"

"Oh, right." Harry selected a file from his top drawer. "I may be the only one left in this world to still use paper files," he mumbled as he opened the file. "A couple of important things happened in the last few days."

Zoe sat up straighter, waiting for the story.

Harry put his reading glasses on. "Last Friday, there was a large explosion in the AI lab, which killed the chief scientist and a couple of security guards."

"Do you mean that John Smith was killed last Friday?" asked Zoe.

"Let me check; yes, the chief scientist's name was John Smith." He lifted his eyes from the paper. "Do you know him?"

"Not personally," said Zoe. "He was my friend's boyfriend's father."

"Oh, sorry for that," said Harry casually.

"Do you suspect that it wasn't an accident?"

"Not sure at the moment. Despite speculations on the news, nobody has claimed responsibility for it yet. We will check the usual suspects. The lab received a few threats from a few religious extremist groups over the years because they believed the lab was interfering with God's work..."

"I know that," interrupted Zoe. "Anyway, this should be a criminal investigation by federal police. It has nothing to do with me, a Taibot agent."

Harry put the paper on his desk, picked up his coffee mug, and sipped slowly. "When you get old, you need this black liquid more than food. All right, the initial investigation revealed that there was a Taibot missing after the explosion."

"A Taibot missing? Last Friday?" asked Zoe in an alarmed voice.

"Yes, it's all here in the file." Harry was too busy looking at the paper to notice the unusual tone in Zoe's voice.

"What kind of Taibot is it?" Recovered from the initial shock, Zoe's voice sounded more or less normal.

"The report doesn't say much about the Taibot." He put down his coffee mug. "That's why you are getting involved. Zoe, you are my best field agent in Taibot-related crimes, so I have to depend on you to carry out this investigation."

"You are just speculating at the moment, and there is no obvious evidence to indicate that the missing Taibot was responsible for the explosion, right?"

"Right, but we have to check it from the Taibot angle because a Taibot was involved," said Harry, who picked up his coffee mug again.

"Harry, in how many cases have we confirmed that Taibots were responsible for whatever crimes were committed? None. It's always humans who either blame Taibots for their own wrongdoings or tried to reprogram their Taibots and it backfired as a result."

"Zoe, you know very well the real reason why we are investigating every single event as long as it involves a Taibot," said Harry.

Zoe sat back, crossing her legs, and felt a bit more relaxed. "Of course I do; we humans are terrified at the possibility of Taibots gaining consciousness and therefore eliminating us from the surface of the Earth. Harry, it's going to be a long time before that happens."

Harry shook his head. "I have a bad feeling about this. Rumours said that the AI lab may have been close to achieving it, and maybe that's why someone decided to blow it up. The missing Taibot could be the one with human consciousness," he said mysteriously.

"I don't know about that, Harry. It seems to me like just another wild goose chase." Zoe tried to sound casual, hoping her boss didn't sense anything unusual in her tone.

"We aren't done yet." Harry fumbled with the file, reading from the paper. "Not very long after the explosion, five people were killed in an underground parking lot in downtown Sydney."

"So?" asked Zoe.

"To be more accurate, four of the five people killed were not humans but Taibots."

"Okay, have we found out anything unusual about these dead Taibots?"

"These dead Taibots were military grade, and were traced back to one of the largest international criminal syndicates, God's Wishes." Harry lifted his eyes from the paper, looking at Zoe.

"Okay, dead Taibots belonging to GW; what do you want me to do?"

"You haven't asked the most important question: how did they get killed?"

Zoe laughed. "Harry, I am a field agent, not a detective, and that's why you, not me, sit behind this desk. Tell me how they were killed."

Harry emptied his coffee mug with a last gulp, and then wiped his mouth with the back of his hand. "There was no firearm involved, and all were killed by either someone's bare hands or knives belonging to the dead Taibots themselves."

"What?" Zoe knew where this was leading. "Did I get this right: you are telling me whoever killed these Taibots is a hand-to-hand combating martial arts expert."

Harry shook his head, speaking slowly. "No human being is capable of killing four military-grade Taibots only with his own bare hands; it's impossible."

"So you are telling me that it's a Taibot who killed these military-grade Taibots, and you think he could be the missing Taibot from the lab after the explosion."

Harry nodded. "Or missing from the lab before the explosion; you are getting there."

"Why do you think this missing Taibot is so important? Just because he could be the one who killed four military-grade Taibots?"

"It's impossible for any Taibot to kill four military-grade Taibots only using his bare hands; the only possibility is that he has gained real human consciousness."

Although she knew the answer, Zoe went on to ask anyway. "How could human consciousness enable the missing Taibot to have more powerful fighting abilities?"

"Because he could actually understand the martial arts, rather than following the sets of rules in his database."

Zoe knew it was time to leave. Otherwise her boss would sense something strange in her behaviour. "Where would you like me to start?"

"Start by reading these reports about the lab explosion and the underground parking lot killings."

Zoe stood up, ready to leave, but Harry spoke again.

"Zoe, I am sorry about you losing your partner, Nick. I've arranged to get you a replacement as soon as possible. For the time being, you will have to work alone. Are you sure you are okay with it?"

"I'll be fine. Thanks for asking."

Toby stood in the living room, staring at the whole-wall TV screen that was replaying the news about the explosion in the AI laboratory last Friday. As he watched images of the collapsed building, fractions of memories flashed in and out of his mind; he had been there, inside the building, walking through the endless corridors. Toby closed his eyes, trying to figure out why he would have memories of the laboratory, but on opening his eyes again, he still had no idea.

Toby couldn't believe that people thought he was a Taibot; he knew he wasn't: he was a human with human consciousness. However, on the other hand, he understood why they would think that way: because of his physicality and impossible self-healing ability. He could be the result of some kind of scientific experiments, and the secrets could be within the AI lab. Yes, he needed to find out more about the laboratory, Toby decided.

He scanned the room and then knew clearly that he couldn't do the research in Olivia's apartment. Whatever his connection was with the laboratory's explosion could implicate her. He didn't want that happening to Olivia.

Thinking about Olivia brought another mystery to his mind. He didn't know how and why he was in the underground parking lot and had tried to save her without even considering if it was possible or not. Toby also couldn't explain how he had the fraction of flashback memory that he'd attended Olivia's family barbecue gatherings before; it was simply impossible, because Olivia obviously didn't know him at all.

He liked Olivia, quite a lot, even knowing almost nothing about her. Much to his delight, she seemed to like him as well. So there were more reasons to avoid harming her in any way. Toby made up his mind; he needed to go out and find a public place to use the Internet.

Toby took the lift down to street level; he didn't order a taxi because he did not want to get unnecessary attention, so public transportation would be a better choice. Walking outside of the air-conditioned building was a harsh test of endurance. It was forty degrees Celsius, and Toby felt the oven-like heat baking him all over. Fortunately a bus stop was only a few blocks away. Even after spending only a few minutes walking, Toby felt like a fish out of water. He didn't know how long he would last if he had to keep walking. It was a wonderful relief when he finally got into the cool and dry air-conditioned metal-and-glass box. It was even better that the bus was free.

Sitting on the top level of the double-decker bus, peering through the tinted glass ceiling, Toby enjoyed the multi-level bands of flying cars overhead and beyond. Since it seemed that buses were the only vehicles running on the streets, there were few traffic jams, so Toby soon arrived at the state library.

The state library was a large square-shaped glass building; the central full-height skylight provided illumination for all the floors around the circular hall. Toby walked to the rows of chest-high benches on the ground floor. As soon as he stopped in front of a green light bulb-like object, a few beams of light emitted from the bench top, intersected, and formed a three-dimensional hologram.

Toby stared at the hologram, with no idea what to do; what happened next surprised him. Without thinking, he put his hand into it, pushing, tweaking, and twisting a few times, until the 3D hologram collapsed into a 2D display on the bench top. He looked at his hands, speechless; he knew what to do after all.

Turning his head around, Toby looked down and quickly typed a few words into the search engine: Artificial Intelligence Laboratory Sydney. Instantly, a stream of results poured onto the display. He stared at the montage of photos of the damaged laboratory for a long time, unsure which photo to select. It must have been a couple of minutes before, out of nowhere, a web address jumped into his head. Without thinking much about it, Toby typed in the address, and a web page appeared.

It was the home page of the AI Laboratory Sydney, judging by its layout and the logo that was displayed. Without thinking, Toby selected the internal login and typed in passwords he didn't know even a couple of minutes ago. Soon a new page appeared.

The page was somewhat familiar; he had seen it before. However, a second set of passwords was required. Toby typed in the password he had typed in earlier, but it didn't work. He retyped it a few times, even trying a combination of capital and lowercase letters, but it was fruitless. As he searched his memory, hoping another set of passwords would jump into his mind, an alarm went off inside the building.

Loud speakers asked everyone to get their IDs ready for checking. By pure instinct, Toby moved away from the benches, joining the crowd walking toward the exit. Large groups of dark uniformed police officers blocked the entrance; they used handheld ID readers to scan each person's wrist.

Toby knew that he'd be caught, as he didn't have his ID with him at the moment. He also knew he couldn't be caught by the authorities or anybody else for extremely important reasons that were lost in his memories. He slowly moved sideways and then walked up to the second floor. While walking, he witnessed a few struggles as the police arrested those who didn't have IDs; he was not sure if they were human or not. Fortunately Toby wasn't the only one walking upward. Most people kept going about their business, as this seemed like a business as usual event.

Only when looking upward did Toby realize that he had reached the top floor; he looked down at the ring of black uniformed police officers, who were getting closer and closer to his floor. Toby knew with certainty that he was trapped and had no way out.

9. Discussions

"Toby, what are you doing here?"

Toby turned around to see Olivia standing behind him. He looked back; the group of police had just reached his floor. "Liv, I can explain it to you later, but you have to get me out of here first; I don't have any ID with me."

Olivia held Toby's arm, leading him toward the elevators. Behind them, the police officers started to ask everyone to show their ID. They were halfway between the police and the elevators.

"We can't get out through the elevator," said Toby quietly.

"I know; I'm just buying us some time. Do you have anything better?"

Toby shook his head, so they walked toward the elevator, trying to be as casual and relaxed as possible.

"Excuse me, madam and sir," a voice called from behind, a police officer's.

They stopped in front of the elevator. Olivia turned around. "What can I do for you, Officer?" asked Olivia.

"I hope you have realized that we are in the process of checking everyone's ID, ma'am," said the police officer, a relatively young male who seemed to have joined the force not that long ago.

"Oh no, I hadn't; I hadn't noticed anything else around except him." Olivia patted Toby's face.

"Ma'am, I have to check your ID," said the young officer.

"No problem." Olivia withdrew her arm from Toby's.

"It won't be necessary," a voice said firmly from behind them.

Olivia closed her eyes momentarily; that was close, very close. She turned. "Zoe."

Zoe walked over, showed her badge to the young officer, and said, "Leave them to me."

"Yes, ma'am." The young officer walked away.

"Liv, what are you and Toby doing here?" asked Zoe.

"I am doing my research; Toby was getting bored at home, so I asked him to come with me," said Olivia.

"Do you guys have your IDs with you?" asked Zoe.

"I do, but Toby forgot his. He's still not quite familiar with how we do things here," said Olivia.

"I am sure there is routine ID checking in the UK as well, is that right, Toby?" Zoe gazed into Toby's eyes.

"Probably." Toby glanced at Olivia, and then added, "I haven't been home for a very long time, so I'm not quite sure about what happens in the UK anymore."

"Zoe, could you please do me a favour and let Toby leave? I have seen his passport and can show it to you later."

After Toby explained what had happened in the state library, Olivia said thoughtfully, "It seems that you definitely had something to do with the AI lab. What are you going to do next?"

"I am not sure if today's ID checking had anything to do with me logging into the lab's web page, but I suspect it did. It was too much to be just a coincidence," said Toby. "The lab is the only thing I know about that gives me any hope of discovering my memories at the moment, so I've decided to visit the lab."

"Visit the lab? Wouldn't it be very dangerous if the police checked the entire library just because you logged into the web page?"

"Yes, I agree, but it's the only thing I can go after right now."

Olivia thought about it for a little longer. "All right, when do you want to do it?"

"Maybe in the middle of the night tonight." Toby suddenly remembered something. "You know, it's so strange that I can suddenly remember the chief scientist's face. From nowhere, his image popped into my mind."

"You must have seen his photo on the Internet after the explosion."

"Maybe," said Toby. "But I have a feeling that I knew him very well; I was related to him closely somehow."

An idea flashed through Olivia's mind. "Wait a moment." She went to her bedroom and brought back a pile of papers. "This was one of the papers John published about artificial intelligence research."

Toby stared at the colour photo printed on the top page. "Yes, that was the chief scientist I suddenly remembered as if I have known him for my whole life. Who's the person next to him?"

"If you did know John for your whole life, you should know about him as well."

"Who's he?" asked Toby.

"He's John Smith's only son, Leo," said Olivia. She watched Toby's expression closely.

"Leo? No, I don't have any memories of him."

Olivia felt a bit disappointed. "I need to show you one more thing." She went to her room again and brought a shoebox back.

Toby watched curiously as she opened the lid. Olivia took out a white envelope. "Inside is a facial mask that will disguise you so that computerized facial identification programs won't recognize you."

Toby took it from her hand and took the skin-coloured mask out of the envelope. "It looks like an ordinary mask."

"Yes, it does," said Olivia. "But it has special features that are able to deceive cameras and programs. Leo invented it for using in online chats when he didn't want to show his real face."

"What about people? Is it able to deceive people's naked eyes?"

"There is only one way to find out. I'll help you to put it on; I did it many times with Leo."

It was just before midnight.

Before Toby went out, Olivia hugged him and then kissed him deeply. It took Toby completely by surprise. The impact was enormous; he suddenly had the exact image jumping into his mind: Olivia held him and kissed him just like she had done right now. How could it be possible? He shook his head in disbelief, and it alarmed Olivia. She quickly released him. "Sorry for doing that."

"Oh no, I like it; there is no need to apologize."

"But you shook your head," said Olivia.

Toby thought about it, and then decided to tell her. "Liv, while you kissed me, I suddenly remembered that you had kissed me in the exact same way before. I know it's impossible."

"It is strange," said Olivia. "Because I haven't lost my memories, so I can vow that I have never kissed you in my whole life."

Toby hugged her back, and then said, "Let's hope that I can find something in the lab and get my memories back. You never know, maybe we knew each other very well in our previous lives."

"Don't tell me you believe in reincarnation?"

"I don't know what my belief was; it's all in the lost memories," said Toby.

Olivia took another piece of thin, transparent film from another envelope and then put it on Toby's left wrist. "This is the ID that comes with the mask; there are sufficient credits in it for your transportation and other purchases as required."

The AI lab was situated quite a way distant from the north side of Sydney harbor. Large parts of the dome-shaped building had collapsed as a result of the explosion. Based on his Internet research, Toby knew that most parts of the building were underground. It was unclear how much damage there was to the underground parts of the lab where the real facilities were. Maybe no reporters were allowed to visit the site after the explosion.

Toby watched the site from quite a distance. Under the pale streetlights, he could see a few security guards patrolling the area, which was protected by temporary wire mesh fences. After watching for another hour or so, Toby was quite confident that he knew enough about the patterns of the security guards and the surveillance cameras' angles and timing, so he decided to take his next step.

As soon as the pair of guards walked around the corner, Toby ran toward the fence soundlessly. He leaped upward, grabbed hold of a tree branch, and landed inside the fence quietly, like a big cat. He crouched down for a couple of minutes until the next pair of guards walked past and the camera moved to the other side of the site, then he entered the ruins from under the gap in the collapsed concrete slabs.

Soon Toby was inside the corridors of the underground part of the lab. He suddenly remembered where to go. He knew these corridors well, and most importantly, he knew the exact location of the chief scientist's office.

There was no light anywhere. Toby closed his eyes for a moment and then opened them again. Gradually he was able to make out where things were. Like some of his other unexplainable abilities, Toby had no idea how he could see in the almost complete darkness.

It was deadly quiet among these maze-like corridors. The crumbled building had cracks to let outside light seep in. It was so weak that for ordinary people it would seem like absolute darkness, but it was sufficient for Toby to get around. Then Toby sensed there was another person in his presence. He hadn't seen or heard anything yet, but he just knew it somehow. He kept walking at the same pace, pretending not to be aware of his possible opponent.

His opponent must have had some kind of tool to track him, maybe a thermal image scanner, because he could neither see nor hear anything, but he knew he was there, following each of his steps but keeping a good distance between them. Toby was very close to his destination now. He stopped, scanning his surroundings.

The office ahead was still intact, so the chief scientist must have been in the working area when the explosion happened. After waiting another five minutes or so, Toby walked over, opened the door, and entered the office. To his relief, as he expected, there was no alarm or other surveillance devices around.

Toby scanned the office; it was completely empty. He opened a few drawers under the desk; there was not even one piece of paper in them. He searched through the entire office, but it was fruitless. Sighing internally, Toby sneaked out of the office and decided to have a look at the damaged parts of the lab.

As soon as he turned around the corner, he sensed the danger was closing in, but it was too late to act.

Lights suddenly switched on.

"Don't move! Lie down on your stomach and put both hands behind your head, now."

Toby sighed and did as ordered.

10. Strangers

Toby raised his hands, put them behind his head, and then slowly lay on his stomach on the floor. Footsteps moved toward him quickly. Without looking up, he knew exactly who the person was. However, he then sensed more people from the other side of the corridor were also approaching them. It appeared that his opponent wasn't aware of the incoming danger. Although it may sound unbelievable, just based on the faint footsteps, Toby knew the approaching party meant harm to both him and his opponent.

"A group of men are coming our way, and they intend to hurt both of us, so please let me help you," said Toby in a calm voice.

"Don't even think about it," said Zoe. She walked a bit closer, pointing her gun at the stranger on the ground. "Who are you? Why are you here?"

"Listen to me carefully. We are both in great danger and could be killed if you don't let me get up and help you," Toby said again.

"Your trick won't work on me. I see and hear no danger anywhere. Cuff yourself, now!" Zoe threw the handcuffs in front of the intruder.

"Take it easy and I'll do exactly what you are asking." Toby slowly moved his hands from behind his head and picked up the handcuffs. He used the opportunity to glance up, and he confirmed his earlier sense. It was Zoe; he had identified her by her smell.

"Hurry up," said Zoe.

"Take it easy." Toby was about to put the handcuff around his left wrist when he heard a cracking sound from the corner of the corridor. Zoe looked up, and that was sufficient for Toby to act. He flung the handcuffs away and knocked Zoe's gun from her hand. Then his body sprang off the ground; he knocked Zoe off her feet, and they landed five feet away.

70

Even before Zoe landed fully on the ground, bullets whistled past her head and would have sunk into her body if she were still standing.

Toby rolled over quickly, gripped Zoe's gun, and fired rapidly. The five newly arrived people fell to the ground. "Give me your spare clips and go," Toby shouted at Zoe, still firing.

Zoe hesitated. "Why do you want to save me?"

"Just go." Toby emptied the ammunition in his gun. "Clips, now."

Zoe threw her spare clips at Toby and ran in the opposite direction along the corridor.

Toby snatched the clips from mid-air, slotted them into his gun, and fired again. He stopped, rolled to the other side of the corridor, and waited.

There was no shooting coming out. Then someone spoke with a strong European accent. "Please don't shoot. We don't want to hurt you. We just want to have a word with you."

"I don't want to have a word with you. Who are you?" Toby tried to keep the conversation going so Zoe would have time to escape.

"Whatever your name is, please listen carefully. I know you are trying to buy some time so the police agent can escape. However, we are not interested in her; we only want to have a few words with you. Please don't make us use force."

"I don't care if you use force as I have a gun here," Toby shouted back.

"I'll give you three seconds to throw your gun down. One, two…"

"All right, I give up." Toby tossed his gun onto the ground.

A group of masked men ran out from the corner. A bag was put over Toby's head and then he was pushed away along the corridor. He heard the leader order his men to take the dead men away and clean up the mess.

After walking for a while, Toby was led up to the ground level. He was then pushed into a car, and it soon rose off the ground and flew away. Despite being unable to see, Toby managed to use his senses to map out which direction he was flying in.

They didn't fly very long. Based on the speed, Toby estimated that they were still in Sydney, not very far from the city centre. He was dragged from the flying car and led into a building. Finally they stopped. The bag was removed from Toby's head.

Toby blinked his eyes, adjusting to the bright light. He was inside a laboratory with white walls and instruments and test tubes all around. A group of armed men stood behind Toby. They were the ones who had kidnapped him; two men stood in front of him. One was in a black suit and the other in a white laboratory coat.

"Dr. Anderson, what do you think about him?" said the dark-suited man with the strong European accent.

Dr. Anderson walked to Toby, using a hand-held device to scan Toby's head. After a while he stopped. "Mr. Logan, he has chips inside his head, but it's not possible to determine if he's a Taibot or not." He spoke with an Australian accent.

"Is there any way you can make the identification?" asked Mr. Logan.

"The only way is to open his skull, but it could damage the package, so it's too risky," said Dr. Anderson.

"Are there any other ways?" asked Mr. Logan.

"We can do a psychological analysis to prove if he has human consciousness, and whether he possesses superhuman and Taibot capabilities or not."

"Mr. Logan," said one of Toby's kidnappers, the attack team leader, who also spoke in a strong European accent. "Sorry for the interruption. He does have superhuman capabilities."

"How do you know that?" asked Mr. Logan.

"Mr. Logan, he killed five of my men with only five bullets," reported the team leader.

"Oh." Mr. Logan turned back to Dr. Anderson. "Does that mean anything to you?"

"Well…" Dr. Anderson thought for a moment and then said, "Humans with implanted chips would be able to achieve such performance; it's not uncommon for top agents. One thing is sure: he definitely has some connection with the government, because the implanted chip technology is only available for a very few government employees, especially for the top agents."

"Yes, I heard about the technology. Why is it so difficult for others to adopt?" asked Mr. Logan.

"The key issue is the chip-human interfacing technology that is owned by Australia's AI laboratory," said Dr. Anderson.

Toby listened to their conversation with great interest. It seemed that nobody in the room had any concerns about discussing this right in front of him. Again, they suspected he was a Taibot. Finally Toby couldn't help but ask, "Excuse me, can anyone tell me what's going on here?"

Dr. Anderson turned to Toby. "What's your name?"

"Why am I here?" asked Toby.

"What were you doing in the lab tonight?" asked Mr. Logan.

"It's not your business. Why did you kidnap me and what do you want from me?" Toby said.

Mr. Logan turned to Dr. Anderson. "It doesn't seem like we are going to get anywhere by talking to him. He's either a stupid man or a very smart Taibot, so it's up to you to figure that out. No drugs on him. I want him unspoiled. I hope you understand this point: unspoiled."

"Of course," said Dr. Anderson. "Take him to the interrogation room."

Two men held Toby's arms behind him and pushed him toward the exit. Just at that moment, Toby took action. He twisted his arms, shaking off the two men's hands, and then quickly grabbed the handgun from one of them. Toby pointed the gun at Mr. Logan.

"I don't know what you want from me and I don't care. Let me go or I'll shoot you," shouted Toby.

Mr. Logan waved his arms to signal to the men behind Toby to lower their guns. "It won't work; nobody will let you go, no matter if you kill me or anyone else. Besides, they'll shoot you in your arms, legs, and other parts of your body to disable you."

Toby put the gun against his own head. "What about killing myself?"

There was real panic in Mr. Logan's face that was absent even when Toby was threating to kill him a moment ago. Toby knew he had pushed the right button; somehow these people thought he was so valuable that even their own lives were unimportant.

"You don't want to do that," said Mr. Logan in a shaking voice, as if Toby was threatening to kill him. "Okay, I will tell you the truth: we suspect that the AI lab succeeded in producing the first ever Taibot with real human consciousness. You can understand the significance to the world and mankind."

"So you believe I am the Taibot and you can sell me for a large amount of money?" said Toby.

"Oh no, far beyond anything money can buy," said Mr. Logan. "But if you truly believe you are just a human, we'll let you go after our analysis."

Toby kept the gun against his own head steadily. "You'd never let me go regardless of the result. If I am the Taibot, the answer is obvious; if not, you'd kill me to keep the crime a secret. So do you want to take the chance of letting me kill myself?"

11. Zoe's Department

Zoe walked into her boss' office.

"Hi, Zoe, I knew you'd be able to get a result," said her boss from behind his large desk.

'Not really." Zoe sat on the guest chair in front of Harry's desk.

"Zoe, how did you know he would visit the lab last night?"

"I didn't, but after someone tried to log into the lab's website with a legit login name and password, I had a hunch he might try to visit the lab."

Her boss drank some of his coffee. "If that's the case, why didn't you bring backup with you?"

Zoe leaned back in her chair. "As I said, it was just a hunch, and I didn't want to embarrass myself if it came to nothing."

Harry paused for a few seconds. "Zoe, how certain are you that he is the one we are after?"

"Not very, but it's possible."

Harry picked up a few pieces of paper from the file on his desk. "Based on this, you only had a very brief interaction with him, so how could you be so certain he wore a mask?"

Zoe patted her head. "Thanks to our government's investment, the chips in my head enable me to make the judgment instantaneously. I sensed his facial expressions weren't as natural as they should be."

"I see," said Harry slowly.

"Harry, if there is nothing else, I'd like to go back and have some sleep. As you can imagine, I didn't get much rest last night."

"Of course," said Harry. "But before you leave, you might be interested to hear this." He took another file out of his top drawer, opening it and picking up a piece of paper. "Despite wearing a mask, he was unable to disguise his footprints. Do you know what we got from his footprints?"

"Just tell me," said Zoe.

Harry sat back, sipping more of his precious coffee. "Do you still remember the killings in the underground parking lot I told you about not long ago?"

"Of course I remember. Are you telling me the guy last night was the same one who killed all five people in the underground parking lot?"

Harry put the piece of paper down. "You bet; the footprints matched perfectly."

"That'd explain a lot," mumbled Zoe to herself.

"Mind sharing with me?" asked Harry.

"Oh." Zoe shook her head, as if jolted back to the real world. "The guy last night was very good in combat; if not for his fast reaction, I'd definitely be dead. He either had chips implanted like me, or he was a Taibot with real human consciousness, and that would explain how he was capable of killing the four military-grade Taibots. But the question is why he didn't kill me, but saved me instead last night?"

Harry shook his head and then engulfed the rest of the black liquid in his cup. He closed the files and then looked at Zoe. "We don't know. Anyway, we are chasing all leads to find out. There is not much you can do at the moment, so why don't you go back to your vacation and have a good rest. I'll keep you informed."

"Oh, thanks, Harry, that's very kind of you." Zoe was ready to leave.

"Ah, Zoe, I almost forgot. I would like you to meet a person." Harry pushed a button on his desk. He smiled mysteriously.

"Who's this person, Harry?"

"You'll know soon enough." Harry stood up, walking around his desk and approaching the door behind Zoe. "Please be seated," said Harry, as Zoe was about to stand up.

Zoe heard the door opening; someone walked in and stood behind her.

"You can turn around now," said Harry.

Zoe stood up, turned, and gasped; the person standing in front of her was Nick. This was impossible, because Nick was dead. He had died in order to save her life. She turned to her boss. "Tell me what's going on here."

"I didn't hear thanks from you," said Harry.

"Harry, tell me."

"Hi, Zoe, I am the replacement for your lost partner Nick," the newcomer said.

Harry shrugged. "We were all sorry for your loss, so I ordered a replacement for you; he's the latest model in his category. What do you think?"

"Harry, I appreciate your kindness, but I don't need another partner, not now."

"Zoe, if you'd had a partner last night, you'd have caught the guy."

Zoe sighed. "All right, we can discuss this after my vacation."

Harry looked at Zoe and spoke firmly. "Zoe, this can't wait until after your vacation."

"What do you mean?"

"You need to take him with you."

"What? I don't want to take him home with me. I didn't even take Nick home."

Harry patted Zoe's arm. "Zoe, this is for your protection. The target may approach you again, so it'd be handy to have a partner watching your back."

"Harry, I don't need anyone watching my back..."

Harry interrupted. "Zoe, this is an order."

Zoe sighed internally. "All right, you are the boss." She turned to her new partner. "Let's get out of here."

"Are you going to call him Nick as well?" asked Harry.

"No." Zoe thought for a second. "James, your name is James."

"Oh, I like James, like James Bond. Pretty cool," said her new partner, who was now named James.

Zoe frowned. She didn't like him at all. Why would they produce a new model of Taibot like this? She turned around and left her boss' office; behind her, James followed closely.

After Zoe left, Harry picked up the phone from his desk. "...yes, James, I mean her replacement partner—she calls him James—went home with her and will watch her 24/7..."

Mr. Logan stared at Dr. Anderson's face, only a few inches away. "How confident are you that he is the one we are after?"

Dr. Anderson laughed drily. "Reasonably." He withdrew a few steps back to his desk. After picking up a remote control and pushing a button on it, an image appeared on the whole-wall TV panel: the dead bodies strewn over the underground parking lot. "These were photos taken from the crime scene by the police."

"I've seen them before," said Mr. Logan impatiently.

"Have a look at this." Dr. Anderson pushed some buttons, and the photo of the person they had captured last night at the lab appeared on the wall. "Although he escaped, I recorded quite a lot of information about him while he was with us."

"Did you establish any connection between him and the underground parking lot killings?" asked Mr. Logan.

"Yes. Based on the footprints from the parking lot, I am quite confident it's him who killed the five people there," said Dr. Anderson.

Mr. Logan turned around, stared at the back of the door for a while, and then said, "Is there any way we can trace him now?"

Dr. Anderson pushed a button, and the underground parking lot photo appeared on the wall again. He pushed a few more buttons and zoomed in on the image, then used computer generated graphics to highlight the footprints in different colours. "As you can see, a pair of footprints is unaccounted for; they likely belonged to a young woman."

"You didn't tell me about this before," said Mr. Logan.

"We only hacked into the police database and obtained this information recently," said Dr. Anderson.

"Are you able to identify the woman by the footprints?" asked Mr. Logan.

"It won't be easy to find her from the few million women living in Sydney, but the police will carry out the investigation for us," said Dr. Anderson.

Mr. Logan turned to the team leader who led the action last night in the lab. "You don't need me to tell you how important it is to capture this guy alive, even if it means losing your life and mine, understand?"

"Of course, Mr. Logan."

Olivia felt the thin film on her wrist vibrating; she glanced down and saw it was Zoe. "Hi, Zoe."

"Hi, Liv, can you enable your image function so I can see you?"

Olivia tapped her wrist a couple of times so Zoe's image appeared on her wall. "What's up, Zoe?"

Zoe looked very tired. "I am back on vacation now."

"How? I thought you were on a big case," asked Olivia.

"I don't know, it's my boss' decision. Anyway, I do need a break. Is Toby still with you?"

"Yeah; he's in the shower at the moment. Do you need to talk to him?"

"Oh no. I just talked to Sophie and Ava about the weekend outing; they both demanded that you take Toby with you for the weekend."

Olivia thought for a moment. "Well, I'll need to discuss it with Toby first."

"No problem. Just let us know soon if he agrees." Zoe hung up.

Toby walked out of the bedroom. "I heard you guys talking."

"What should we do?"

12. Conversations

Olivia and Toby took a flying ship to the weekend retreat place. Zoe wasn't able to go with them, but she said that she'd arrive around dinnertime.

The retreat place was a few hundred kilometres away from Sydney on the coastline. While flying, Olivia didn't talk much but watched the landscape beneath them, where the vast farmlands that used to be there had turned into desert. They flew for a long time before seeing something green. Finally they landed.

Due to its location on the Australian continent, the temperature here was tolerable for the trees and grass to grow. However, the retreat area was restricted to a bare minimum, as every possible acre of food-producing land was used for crops. It was lucky that Sophie won the ballot last year so they had a spot for the weekend.

In fact, the retreat area was relatively large. If one only stayed within a few miles of the retreat, one would have no idea that most of the rest of Australia had turned into desert. It was a relatively short walking distance from the flying ship landing station to their accommodation.

The front door was open. It seemed that the others had arrived not long ago, as the unpacked suitcases were still lying around the living area. Olivia put down her luggage and shouted, "Soph, long time no see."

A woman with dyed blue hair standing behind the kitchen bench turned around. "Wow, Liv, long time no see, indeed. How are you!" She hugged Olivia.

"I'm all right. Soph, this is Toby. Toby, Soph, my friend from uni," said Olivia.

Toby and Sophie shook hands and exchanged pleasantries. Sophie was five foot seven with a yoga practitioner's body; based on her accent, she must be from London originally.

No sooner had Toby let go of Sophie's hand than a woman rushed out of the corridor. "My God, it's you, Liv!" Even before Olivia opened her mouth to say anything, the newcomer, who had dirty-blond hair and a heavy five-foot-eleven build, bear-hugged Olivia tightly. It lasted a few seconds that must have seemed like an eternity to the struggling Olivia. Finally, a little out of breath, Olivia said, "Ava, this is Toby; Toby, Ava, also my uni friend."

"Nice to meet you, Ava." Toby shook Ava's hand. She was fit and must work in an occupation involving lots of physical activity.

"Nice to meet you, too." Ava held Toby's hand a second longer than she should. After tearing her gaze from Toby's, she turned in the direction of the corridor. "Luke, my dear, come here to meet my friends."

Luke was six foot two, with a slender build and blond hair. Ava introduced him as a twenty-year-old university student. After Luke shook hands with Olivia and Toby, Olivia said, "Ava, you've been through quite a few boyfriends recently, but I don't recall you ever having a firefighter one."

"Yeah. Now you mention it, I am beginning to wonder about it myself." Ava thought about it for a moment. "Possibly because I deal with them every day, so I don't need one in my bedroom as well. Maybe one day I'll get on it."

So Ava was a firefighter. Toby nodded but said nothing.

"Michael, please meet my friend Liv and her friend Toby!" Sophie said pleasantly.

While shaking hands with Michael, Toby observed both Luke and Michael with great interest; so they were the human companion type Taibots. Michael was a fifty-five-year-old professor and Luke a football player in university. From the brief interactions, he realized they could easily pass as human based on their intelligence.

"Liv, Toby has a great body, even better than Luke's. If I didn't already know Toby was a human, I'd definitely think he was a Taibot," said Ava.

"Not only does he have a perfect body, from my brief interaction with him, Toby is also a good talker with a sense of humour as well," said Sophie.

"Well, as I've told you many times, Toby and I are really only friends at this stage." Olivia knew exactly what was in their minds. Ava and Sophie obviously believed that Olivia had finally bought a Taibot boyfriend but was too embarrassed to admit it so claimed Toby was a human. She wished she knew the answer to the question, too.

Their accommodation was a large five-bedroom farmhouse, quite spacious. As discussed and agreed upon, Sophie and her boyfriend Michael and Ava and her boyfriend Luke would occupy a bedroom each, while Toby and Zoe's partner James had a room each for themselves. Olivia and Zoe would share the last room.

It was late afternoon, so after everyone had put their luggage away, the boyfriends started to prepare dinner while the ladies put their feet up and enjoyed a glass of white wine, a rare special treat since there was not much land left for growing grapes.

From the balcony under the veranda, one had a view of the front yard: green plants along the farmhouse, with tiny white flowers dotting the edge. On the other side of the narrow walkway, taller trees shielded the residence from the outside world. It was one of the last cosy, calm, and picturesque country living paradises, and it would soon disappear forever.

"It's so unusual for a great guy like Toby to like cooking," said Ava. "I'd definitely believe he was a Taibot if I didn't already know better."

"Well, it is rare, particularly nowadays, but obviously they do exist." Sophie turned to Olivia. "Liv, how lucky you were to bump into Toby. If I were you, I'd do whatever I could to keep him."

"Er, what? Of course." Olivia wasn't really listening to their conversation but was immersed in her own thoughts.

"Never mind." Sophie turned to Ava and chatted about other things.

From what Toby had told her about his adventure in the collapsed AI laboratory building, Olivia knew there was a large and complicated story behind Toby's lost memories. It was understandable why Zoe was there and almost caught Toby, and fortunately Toby saved Zoe's life, but what puzzled Olivia, and Toby, was the third party involved. It seemed likely that these people were some kind of criminal organization, but Olivia just couldn't understand why Toby was so important that they'd willingly let him go when he threatened to kill himself. These questions ran around in her mind, but she was unable to make any sense out of them.

"Liv, what are you thinking about?" asked Ava.

Olivia looked up at Ava. "Nothing really, just a bit tired; I didn't sleep very well last night."

Ava glanced at Toby. "Who would need sleep when you have such a gorgeous guy in your bedroom?"

"Liv and Toby are just friends," said Sophie with a grin.

"I know what's in your dirty minds." Olivia looked out onto the balcony and saw Zoe walking toward them; the guy walking beside her must be James, Zoe's new partner. "Look who is coming."

James was about six foot, with a slick athletic body without too many muscles. He wasn't the handsome type some girls would prefer, but he was definitely Zoe's type. Although everyone had speculated and joked about Zoe's relationship with her previous partner, Nick, Zoe had never brought Nick home, so Olivia had never actually met Nick. Under the circumstances, Zoe had asked Olivia not to mention anything to the others about what had happened to Nick.

James was quite charming with the ladies. He wasn't much of a domestic kind of guy, so he didn't do much in the kitchen to help the other males to prepare the dinner, instead spending large chunks of time talking to Ava and Sophie, who were obviously enjoying his company.

Zoe sat down on the sofa in the living area. Olivia walked over to her. "Can I get you something to drink?"

"Maybe a beer; I still have a few beer coupons to use up," said Zoe while putting her feet up on top of the coffee table.

After she had settled down a bit, Olivia sat beside Zoe. "James seems quite charming. A ladies' man, I would say."

"I would agree with you," said Toby, who placed a plate of cheese and crackers on the coffee table.

Zoe turned around, glancing at James, who was chatting with Ava and Sophie on the balcony. "No matter how smart or charming James seems to be, he's just a Taibot, after all; unlike you, Toby, a real human male."

"Well, Taibots are so advanced nowadays, sometimes it's hard to tell the difference, don't you think?" Toby went back to the kitchen again.

After dinner, Zoe said to James, "Liv and I are going to go for a walk nearby."

"I need to go with you," said James.

"No, you don't," said Zoe.

"It's my duty to protect you; I can't let you out of my sight," said James.

"Really?" Zoe gazed at James. "Who's the boss here, you or me?"

"Of course you are the boss, ma'am," said James.

Zoe and Olivia walked along the footpath outside of the retreat accommodation area. Due to ground vehicles disappearing, there were no highways anywhere, particularly in these valuable farming lands. Zoe took a deep breath. "I love fresh air with the smell of green plants. I wonder how long we will be able to enjoy this."

"I am afraid not as long as we hope for," said Olivia.

It was an early dinner, and the sun still hovered a few feet above the horizon. They walked on the long jetty that stretched out into the natural bay. A large pelican stood on top of a tall street light pole, appearing as a black silhouette in the blood red light from the sinking sun.

They were quite a distance from any potential eavesdropping. Zoe stopped and then turned around, facing Olivia. "We need to watch each other's backs while talking," she said in a quiet voice.

Olivia looked at the water beneath the jetty they were standing on and then said quietly, barely audible above the noise of the waves pounding the seashore, "Are you worried someone may be monitoring or listening to our conversation?"

"You can never be too careful," said Zoe. "Liv, tell me, how did you and Toby meet?"

Olivia sensed the seriousness in Zoe's tone. "I told you that we bumped into each other on the street..."

"Liv," interrupted Zoe. "I know you lied to me when you told me that the first time, and now I need to know the truth. It's far more serious and important than you could ever imagine."

Olivia shook her head. "You know I am hopeless at lying, particularly in front of my best friend."

"I am listening," said Zoe.

"Well, things started that Friday evening on my way home. I noticed a young man who was sitting under a doorway; initially I thought he was just homeless, but he seemed to recognize me and starting to approach me, so I panicked and ran away." Olivia took a deep breath and then continued. She told Zoe how she was kidnapped and dragged into the underground parking lot.

"Underground parking lot? By five men?" Zoe interrupted. "How did you know?"

"I'll tell you later. Tell me what happened next," said Zoe.

Olivia told Zoe how she had faced her attackers and believed it would be the end of her life, and then the young man appeared. She recounted how the young man had fought the five men and killed them; how she helped him back to her apartment; how she discovered that he had lost his memories due to the head injury from the fighting; how she was amazed and suspicious about how quickly he recovered from his injuries. She also told Zoe about Toby's adventure in the AI lab.

"That's the true version of my story," said Olivia.

Zoe thought for a long time and then nodded. "That explains a lot."

"Explains a lot about what?"

"As we all know, despite Taibots becoming so sophisticated and smart that it's difficult to tell the difference between them and real humans, they don't have real human consciousness. Since true AI emerged ten years ago, artificial consciousness has become the next holy grail everyone is desperately searching for. You know why?" said Zoe.

"Another scientific breakthrough," said Olivia wearily. "I don't believe it's possible though."

"Not many do except one person, John Smith," said Zoe. "Anyway, the significance of artificial consciousness is that it'd enable the next evolution: the evolution from human to machine transformation."

"Yeah, I know that, but it's just a theory. It's impossible for machines to obtain human consciousness."

"That's what everyone believes. But on the eve of humanity being wiped out by global warming, many regard artificial consciousness as our only salvation, the only hope of keeping intelligence alive, intelligence that very probably exists nowhere else in the universe," said Zoe.

Olivia stared at the now darkened waves for a while. "So everyone, including you, believes that Toby is the Taibot with true human consciousness?"

"Don't you?" Zoe gazed at Olivia.

"As I said, I did have my suspicious and doubts about whether he was a Taibot or not; however, there are more unexplainable things." Olivia told Zoe about Toby having those memories of being with her. "Zoe, is there any chance that Leo's father, John Smith, somehow created Toby, and also transplanted Leo's memories into him as well?"

"If Toby is a Taibot, then anything is possible. We'd need to test and prove if he has human consciousness first," said Zoe.

"No need for that. I can confirm he's a real human for sure."

"How do you know that? We assess and judge if other human beings are conscious or not based on the assumption that all humans have the same physical structures in our heads, but this wouldn't be true for a Taibot," said Zoe.

"Are you telling me that human psychology can't be used to assess Taibots?"

Zoe nodded.

"So what can we use then?"

"No one has a clue about this." Zoe moved even closer to Olivia. "I am under oath that I won't tell this to anyone. Do you know what the real purpose of my job is?"

Olivia shook her head.

"I am one of the top agents who hunt for artificial consciousness. To investigate Taibot-related crimes is just my cover," said Zoe. "You can imagine the significance of artificial consciousness to any nation or organization. That's why whoever kidnapped Toby let him go rather than endangering his life."

"Zoe, tell me how you became suspicious of Toby. You couldn't know it was Toby in the lab because he wore a mask then."

"Well, I could tell that you didn't tell me the truth about how you and Toby met, and of course his perfect body is a big clue. It's true, I didn't know Toby was the intruder in the lab that night. However, the investigators found a pair of unknown footprints belonging to a young woman, so for me to confirm my suspicions was quite simple and straightforward: matching Toby's and your footprints to the footprints found in the underground parking lot and the AI lab."

Olivia looked worried. "If you could figure this out, so could others."

"Yes, but it'd take them a bit longer because they would need to match a few million footprints. Besides, I don't think they have your footprints in the database."

"So what should we do?" asked Olivia.

"We need to observe Toby and try to find out if he's a Taibot with real human consciousness."

"Then what? Are you going to hand him over to the government?" asked Olivia.

"I don't know. Although it's my duty to do so, it's becoming more complicated as time passes. Now he's somehow related to you, and he also saved my life, so let's wait and see. I think we should go back before the others become suspicious."

"It seems that you don't like James much," said Olivia as they turned back toward their accommodation.

"I don't trust him; I suspect that he was sent to monitor me. They must be suspicious after the event in the lab. They didn't believe my report of the event."

13. Vacation

They went to the vineyard the next morning. It was one of the few grape-growing locations allowed to be kept on the Australian continent that was deemed not suitable for crops. These vineyards produced all the wine for the country's thirty million residents, who were mostly squeezed into the island of Tasmania.

Although May was supposedly the cooler season, at lunchtime the temperature had climbed up to forty degrees Celsius. It was too hot to sit outside. However, the sweeping view of the vineyard through the glass wall was very impressive, so one couldn't really complain too much in the comfort of the dry and cool air blowing out of the central air-conditioning unit.

Olivia's friends and their male partners sat around the long table that was carved out of a giant tree trunk, made by chopping the upper part of the large log into a flat table top. She stroked the smooth wood body, feeling so sad that there were no such large trees left alive on the continent anymore; it didn't take long for them to become extinct.

As was their tradition, a girl had to sit between two guys but not next to her own partner. Ava's boyfriend, Luke, sat on Olivia's left, and Sophie's, Michael, on her right.

"Liv, I can't believe how much Toby knows about cooking. You are such a lucky girl to have a human boyfriend like him." Ava turned to Toby, who sat next to her, and patted his cheek.

Olivia saw the real embarrassment on Toby's face. She exchanged a look with Zoe and said, "You can say that again; I have been enjoying his culinary skills since we first met."

"Toby, tell us how you guys met," said Sophie, who sat on the other side of Toby.

"I thought Liv told you girls already," said Toby, smiling with an uneasy expressions on his face.

"But we want to hear it from your mouth, darling." Ava patted Toby on his other cheek.

Olivia saw redness rising on Toby's face; it shocked her because Leo would have the same reaction in really embarrassing situations, although it was quite rare. Glancing over, Olivia noticed Zoe was watching the situation with great interest.

"Ava, please keep your hands off Toby," said Luke. "It's not only making Toby feel embarrassed, it's also making Liv and me jealous."

"Oh, no, Toby and I are only friends, so I don't feel jealous at all." Olivia suddenly had an idea. She turned, held on to Luke's neck, and kissed him on his mouth. "Tastes like Irish. So we are even now, Ava, right?"

"No, we are not even at all." Ava grinned and glanced at Toby's mouth sideways. "Toby, just remember that you owe me a kiss. Okay, tell us how you and Liv met."

Although Luke said he felt jealous, Olivia knew it was just the result of his program reasoning and calculating based on the database in his head, so it was no surprise that the supposed jealousy didn't show on his face at all; one could argue that he was joking about it. On the other hand, she saw the complex expressions on Toby's face when she kissed Luke. Behind the forced laughter, she could see a hint of hidden jealousy, a true human emotion.

"Well, not much to say, really." Toby drank a bit of water from the glass in front of him. "Liv and I bumped into each other, literally, on the street."

"Who bumped into whom first?" Sophie laughed.

"I want to know how you guys bumped into each other; which parts of your bodies?" Ava laughed even louder.

"Liv, I remember it was you who ran into me first," said Toby while looking at Olivia.

"I can't remember the details. Who cares anyway," said Olivia.

"What happened after the bumping?" asked Zoe, who joined the conversation for the first time.

Olivia picked up her wine glass. "Toby, you tell them what happened."

"Well, we apologized to each other and talked a bit; we then chatted a bit more. After learning that I was on a backpacking vacation and looking for somewhere to stay, Liv kindly invited me to stay with her for a few days," said Toby, who became more relaxed.

"Wow, I wish I had such a romantic encounter," said Sophie.

"My dear, we do have our moments together," said Michael.

"Of course we do, my dear Michael. I don't mean we don't," said Sophie.

"I thought that Toby and Liv were just friends, right?" James spoke for the first time.

"Yes, James, that's what Olivia said not long ago. What's your point?" Zoe turned, looking at James.

"If they are just friends, it'd be incorrect for Sophie to say it was a romantic encounter," said James expressionlessly.

"So what's the problem, smarty pants?" said Zoe.

"No problem, ma'am." James turned to Toby. "Toby, can I ask you a question?"

"By all means, go ahead," said Toby.

"Unlike you, I am just a Taibot. However, even I understand that cooking skills are not something for a real man to brag about. You are a real man, aren't you?" asked James.

Toby glanced at Olivia briefly; in the short moment their eyes met, she saw the angry flare in his gaze, and then she heard Toby speak calmly.

"James, you are absolutely right, there is nothing to brag about in my cooking skills. Nowadays it's getting harder to tell if one is a real man, don't you think?"

Before James spoke again, Ava put her hand over James' mouth. "I think you are a real man, too."

So the conversation broke up and everyone started talking to the next person.

"Soph, what do you think is the real cause of global warming?" Toby asked, setting down his knife and fork on his empty plate.

"Capitalism, of course!" Sophie picked her glass up, sipping a bit of wine.

"So you believe capitalism destroyed the environment, caused air pollution, is the root of basically all the problems society has, and led to global warming and eventually the demise of humanity?" Toby also sipped a bit of his wine.

"Yes, I do. If we had an alternative system..."

Zoe interrupted. "Do you mean communism? You always say the same thing each time."

"Soph's parents belonged to the Communist Party in the UK," Ava whispered in Toby's ear.

Sophie put her wine glass down. "I know communism didn't work out well in Russia; the Russians weren't able to compete with capitalism from the West, but they didn't destroy the environment and cause the sixth mass extinction."

"We've debated this point many times before, but I want to say it again: there is nothing wrong with capitalism itself. It's a very good system that can encourage innovation and create large amounts of wealth, but the problem is that corruption distorted it, and governments around the globe, particularly in the US, failed to include the environmental costs in the equation," said Zoe.

"You can say that again. In the eighties, the collapse of socialism in the UK and the US basically sealed humanity's fate," said Sophie.

"But I still believe it was the governments' failure to regulate the fossil fuel industry. The government let them get away with polluting the environment because of the powerful fossil fuel lobbies controlling US politicians. If the US government put a tax on carbon dioxide emissions in the eighties, or even the nineties, humanity would have some chance to survive," said Zoe.

"I think it's far beyond that: western individualism is the fundamental cause of all the world's problems," said Olivia.

"What do you mean?" asked Toby.

"Well, unlike collectivism, where all people work for the good of the community, individualism emphasizes individuals' needs; as a result, no one cares about the needs of the world as a whole. Basically, many people, particularly in the US, are still limited to the tribe mentality, unable to see beyond their own interests, so here we are, in the death spiral of environmental disaster." Olivia laughed bitterly.

"I don't disagree with all of your opinions, but the real problem is us, in here." Ava pointed at her head.

"You mean human intelligence?" Toby asked.

"Yes, indeed." Ava gulped a large mouthful of beer and then said, "We kill more animals than we can eat, we wipe out forests so we can eat more meat, and we poison the land with chemical fertilizer so we can produce more food to feed ever-growing populations. Even if we manage to reduce CO_2 in the air and avoid the worst outcome of climate change, the sixth mass extinction caused by loss of bio-diversity, the acidification of the oceans, and the collapse of the food chain would still seal humanity's fate."

"So you are saying human intelligence caused all of those problems. If that's the case, why did humans develop the type of consciousness that destroys humans themselves?" asked Toby.

"Good question indeed," Olivia said. "We thought we were so clever that we could destroy whatever we liked, but we were dumb enough not to realize the consequences."

"I have to agree with you on that point," said Sophie. "Even today, fossil fuel companies are still drilling in ice-free Arctic waters, just like a lung cancer patient taking a last drag of his cigarette on his deathbed."

Ava looked around the table and then said, "I suppose it's not necessarily a bad thing: the extinction of dinosaurs led to the rise of humanity, so the demise of humanity might bring peace to future Earth. Let's hope another conscious being doesn't appear on Earth, at least not one as dumb as humanity."

Toby nodded and didn't ask one more question until the end of the meal.

After they walked out of the restaurant, thick clouds covered the sky and heavy rain poured down. They stood under the veranda, enjoying the cool relief. Although the rain didn't last very long, the overcast sky made the temperature drop quite significantly compared to the scorching heat in the morning.

"Guys, it's rare to have a cool day like this, so why don't we go and do some outdoor activities? Anyone interested in horse riding?" Ava said after the rain stopped.

Everyone agreed, so they walked to the horse riding station next to the vineyard.

The grass, bushes, and trees seemed refreshed and lush after the rainfall. Olivia rode beside Toby. They were riding on the beach, alongside the fences of the vineyard, which was not far away. Behind, Zoe rode beside James while Ava rode with Luke and Sophie with Michael, leading the way.

"That was really a lovely lunch," said Toby.

"It was. This is just wonderful; I haven't been out to enjoy such cool weather for a very long time." Olivia stretched her arms out and leaned her head back, as if embracing the whole sky.

Suddenly, from nowhere, a fork of lightning sliced the overhead clouds, and thunder cracked down at them. Olivia's horse jumped up, threw her out of the saddle, and galloped away. One of Olivia's feet was caught in the stirrup, so her body was dragged and bumped along the sand dunes.

14. New Game

Toby used his palm, hitting his horse hard, chasing Olivia closely. Behind, Zoe and James also zoomed in fast. In fact, it'd only taken a few seconds for Toby to get close to Olivia. He leaped off his horse, flew across the two-meter gap, and landed on Olivia's horse.

Pulling its reins, Toby held the horse back. The horse stood on its hind legs, kicking its front legs high in the air, and then fell, landing on the sand dune. Toby jumped off the horse before its body touched the sand. He quickly untangled Olivia's foot from the stirrup and pulled her away from the horse.

Toby quickly checked Olivia from head to toe.

"Is she all right?" Zoe jumped off her horse.

"No broken bones, just some scratches," said Toby without looking up.

"Are you okay, Liv?" Zoe kneeled beside Olivia and held her hands.

"I am okay, a bit shocked, but I am okay. Where did the fucking thunder come from?" said Olivia.

"I'm so glad you are okay." Zoe held Olivia's head, kissing her forehead. "The fucking thunder indeed." Zoe laughed with relief.

"It seems that the horse has broken its leg," said James from behind.

"What?" Olivia pushed Toby away, standing up.

"Are you all right, Liv?" Ava and Sophie also caught up with them.

"I am okay; just a few scratches." Olivia walked to the horse, which was lying down on the sand dune. "James, how do you know it broke its leg?"

James stood up. "I just checked."

"Oh shit. It's my fault," said Olivia.

"It's not your fault, Liv. If it's anyone's fault, it should be mine because I brought it down," said Toby.

"It's nobody's fault, just an accident." Zoe turned to James. "Are you able to fix its leg?"

"Yes, but I need a stick to stabilize its bones," said James.

"I'll go and get one for you." Toby walked to the vineyard fence and brought a wooden stick back.

"Toby, you need to hold this leg while I put the bones together," said James.

It took Toby a few seconds to make out the sentence. "Sorry, James, I don't think I can."

Olivia could see that Toby felt the pain the horse felt at the moment; watching his expression, she could feel him wince internally.

"What do you mean you can't? Just hold its leg while I am fixing it," said James.

"Luke, could you please help James," asked Olivia gently.

"Of course." Luke walked forward and held the leg while James did his work. It didn't take long for James to put the broken bones together and then secure the leg with the wooden stick. When he was finished, James stood up, looking at Toby. "You humans are so weak."

"Empathy is not a weakness, James, and it should be in your database, too," said Zoe.

"Sorry, ma'am, I don't want to be contradictory, but you humans' greatest weakness is that you can't separate yourselves from your biological instincts."

"We call them compassion, empathy, and love, things that you are not capable of feeling." Zoe looked up, seeing a flying ship coming toward them to rescue them.

They went back to their accommodation. As agreed, nobody was allowed to watch TV or use any Internet devices, as the weekend retreat was purely for human to human, or human to Taibot communication purposes. So after dinner,

Zoe announced, "Girls, since we all have partners with us, human or not, I propose we have a partner quiz night..."

"Who will ask the questions?" Ava interrupted.

"Where will you get the question list from?" asked Sophie.

"Hang on for a moment please, girls." Zoe put her hands up. "I don't have a question list. I propose that, for each round, all the girls take turns to ask a question, so you may want to discuss with your partner what questions would be most advantageous for your partner to answer."

"Any limitations on the questions?" asked Ava.

"No, but we'd prefer not to listen to your bedroom stories," laughed Zoe.

Olivia didn't say anything, just watching and listening to what was happening around her. She knew what Zoe was trying to achieve here, so she thought really hard about what kind of questions she should ask. Looking at the excited expressions on Ava and Sophie's faces, Olivia knew they were obviously in game mode and wanted their Taibot boyfriends to win. She then glanced at Toby, who sat there silently. What was in his mind right now? Olivia was wondering. Toby seemed to behave like a human being in every way, at least from her point of view. This afternoon, when facing the injured horse situation, Toby showed obvious empathy that James did not, but was empathy equal to consciousness? Olivia didn't know and doubted there was a clear and agreed definition for it. Just as she was becoming immersed in her own thoughts, Olivia heard Ava speak loudly.

"Ladies, round one of partners' quiz night. I'll ask the first question. Gentlemen, use the pen and paper in front of you to write down the answers. The question is..."

"Hang on," Zoe interrupted. "Sorry, girls, we need to change the rules a bit. Your partner is not allowed to answer your question. Otherwise, if you ask about a secret only you two know about, it wouldn't be much fun for the rest of us."

"That's not fair; we just spent so much effort on working out our questions," protested Ava.

"Never mind, we'll just go back to the drawing board again," Sophie said, and then started her discussion with Michael.

Olivia saw Zoe didn't talk to James at all. She spoke quietly to Toby, who sat next to her. "Toby, any suggestions?"

"Oh," said Toby, as if suddenly waking up from his deep thoughts. "Suggestions about what?"

Olivia stared at him for a moment, and then said quietly, "Toby, were you listening to what is going on here? We are having a partners' quiz night. The girls will ask questions and their partners will answer them."

"Of course, I was aware of that, but the quiz hasn't started yet, right?" said Toby in an equally low voice.

"That's correct. Toby, do you have any suggestions about what kind of questions I should ask everyone? Every girl will take turns asking questions," said Olivia.

Toby thought for a second. "I have no idea; just ask whatever. Does it really matter?"

"I guess not." Olivia glanced in Zoe's direction; Zoe just sat there and had no intention of talking to James.

"Ladies, are you ready to get the ball rolling?" asked Zoe impatiently.

"We are ready," shouted Ava with her arm looping around Luke's neck.

"So are we," said Sophie while smiling at Michael mysteriously.

"In that case, let's get the game started," announced Zoe. "I'll ask first. Five children play on a live track, and they know there is a danger that a train may come. Nearby a child plays on a disused track, and he also knows it is a safe place to be. A passenger train suddenly appears and is about to kill the five kids. You are by chance standing between the children and the train, and could flip a switch to divert the train to the disused track to kill one child but save the other five. Would you flip the switch and why?"

Luke spoke immediately. "I would flip the switch to save more lives."

Ava patted Luke's cheek. "That's my boy, answering the question fastest and most correctly."

Zoe turned to Michael. "Michael?"

"Flipping the switch is an immoral decision. The child chose to play on the disused track because he is sensible and takes precautions, so why should he have to pay the price for those careless kids' mistakes? I wouldn't flip the switch."

"Interesting," said Zoe, who then turned to Toby. "What do you think, Toby?"

"Wu Wei," said Toby.

"Sorry?" said Zoe.

Olivia looked at Toby and then turned to Zoe. "Wu Wei is a Taoist term. Some simply interpret it as inaction, but that is incorrect. It means to act according to nature's laws rather than against them." Olivia felt that she had done her father a huge credit to be able to say something about such a complex philosophical question in the field he had dedicated his life to.

"What kind of answer is that?" James stood up and shouted at Toby from behind Olivia.

"James, you sit down and shut up," said Zoe.

"Toby, you have to choose, to flip or not to flip the switch." James ignored Zoe.

"In the real world, it's not always a matter of a simple right or wrong answer; it would all depend," said Toby slowly.

"In this case, you would have to choose: kill the one or five kids." James stepped forward, standing beside Olivia.

"James, go back to your seat and shut up, now!" Zoe shouted.

Toby waved his arm. "It's okay, and I'll answer the question. Both choices are right and wrong at the same time, so whatever you chose could be right or wrong."

"But you still have to make the choice, don't you?" asked Ava.

"Yes, and you have to decide if you want to save more lives or make an ethical decision. Through human history, even only recently, how often have we caused the worst catastrophes with the best intentions at the time?" Toby looked around the room, speaking softly and slowly.

"It may sound all right, but it is good for nothing if you don't take action and do something. Toby, what's your answer?" asked James loudly.

Olivia was amazed to see the angry expression on James' face. It was quite unusual for a Taibot to behave like this. She glanced at Zoe, who was frowning. Olivia stood up. "James, let's skip this question. It's my turn to ask next."

What happened next took everyone by surprise. James suddenly used his large hands to grip Olivia's neck. Olivia gasped for air and struggled to keep her balance while being dragged back by James.

Toby jumped up on his feet by pure instinct. Olivia's scared and desperate expression hit him like a bullet. He felt a momentary explosion inside his head, as if he had been struck with a large club. He had to lean back and hold the back of the chair to keep himself steady. Toby blinked his eyes, focusing on the scared woman in front of him, and gradually another similar scene emerged in his mind: it was in the underground parking lot, and the same woman was surrounded by five large guys. He smiled. "You are Olivia. I remember now."

Olivia felt the hand gripping her neck loosen a bit so she could breathe more easily. Looking at Toby's expression, she knew exactly what had just happened; of course, it made absolutely no sense to the rest. A quick glance around the room confirmed her feeling. She smiled, feeling like a mountain of burden had been removed from her back. "Toby, I am so glad."

"James, release her now. This is my order," said Zoe.

"Toby, answer the question. Would you flip or not flip the switch?" James stared at Toby, ignoring Zoe.

Toby raised his arms up. "Take it easy, James. I'll answer the question, but before that, I would like to hear your choice."

'I'd flip the switch," said James.

"Why?" Toby asked.

"Because it would save more lives. Don't you think it'd be better to save five and only kill one?" asked James sarcastically.

"What about the ethical dilemma, killing the innocent?" Toby asked.

"It's necessary to make a sacrifice sometimes in order to achieve greater good," said James.

"Right." Toby thought for a second. "James, do you really think I'd believe you, a Taibot, came up with this idea by yourself?"

James tightened his grip on Olivia's neck a bit to coax more gasping noises out of her mouth, and then released her to let her breath normally. "You know well that I can easily break her neck with just a little squeeze. So now answer my question: would you flip the switch?"

"James, I know you are the latest top model, above even military grade, so why don't you let her go, and we can sort this out between you and me?" Toby said calmly.

"Ha, you want to be the real man, the knight in shining armour who rescues the princess? Okay, I'll grant your wish." James turned to Luke and Michael. "You two, come here."

Olivia was so relieved that Toby had finally got his memories back. She wasn't sure if he had all of his memories back, but it seemed like he could at least remember who she was now. There were so many questions she desperately wanted to ask him right now, but this damn Taibot had forced Toby into a fight situation. Based on her experience from the past few days, she knew that Toby was far more important than anyone in the world, even if she had no clue why that was. "James, please let Toby go, and I'll do anything you want. Please just don't hurt Toby."

Toby put his hands up. "Liv, please don't worry. I can handle the situation. Trust me." He then turned to James. "Let's get to it, the sooner the better."

"What are you doing, Luke?" Ava tried to stop Luke from walking away from her, but Luke forced her back into her chair.

"Ava, let him go," Zoe said in a worried voice.

When both Michael and Luke stood in front of James, he ordered, "Michael, you go ahead and challenge Toby."

"Michael is an English gentleman and has never fought with anybody. He's a philosopher, for God's sake," said Sophie.

"Philosopher, eh?" James sneered. "Michael, show her your martial arts skills."

Michael started shaking his shoulders, as if dancing to music in his head, and then he started to take his top off in a professional stripper fashion.

"That must be the newest style of martial arts to exist, so I don't think I am capable of fighting against it," said Toby.

People in the room laughed nervously, though it did little to break the tension.

"Go back to your mistress, you useless piece of machine." James turned to Luke. "You grip her neck like this, and kill her if anyone tries to save her." After swapping positions with Luke, James moved to the middle of the room. Chairs had been shifted to the corners, and everyone moved to stand along the wall.

15. Farmhouse

James stood in the middle of the room and signalled Toby to come forward. Toby shook his head. "There is not enough room here; we could hurt bystanders. Why don't we go outside?"

So it was settled. While Luke dragged Olivia, leading the way with his hand still gripping her neck, James, Toby, Zoe, and the rest followed them to the backyard. The well-lit barbecue area provided an almost perfect arena for the upcoming gladiator-style fighting.

"Toby, it seems you have sufficient confidence to face an above military grade top model Taibot, so the question is if you are a real human, because no human has such a capability," James said without much expression on his face, as if reading the text from an invisible TV screen.

"I don't really want to fight, but I don't want Liv getting hurt either, so here we go." Toby walked to the centre of the grassy area, and the fighting started.

As stated, James was true to his capabilities. His attacks were fast, ferocious, and accurate. It seemed that his combating program must have collected the best parts of all the martial arts that had ever existed and then poured them into the chip in his brain. In contrast, Toby was more like a shadowy figure, floating around and just managing to evade the blows at the last possible moment. James' palm missed Toby but chopped at a tree branch nearby. The dinner plate-thick branch cracked clear off the trunk. The bystanders kept moving backward, pressing against the wall as hard as they could to avoid being hit by the fast-moving pair.

It felt like ages, but in fact, Toby delivered his first and last blow just after the half-minute mark. Toby turned his body sideways, letting the punching fist pass his cheek narrowly; his elbow struck James' chest. Toby kept his body twisting, and the edge of his palm chopped at James' neck; the sickening cracking sound declared that James was beyond repair.

The following silence sank slowly into everyone's mind, but before anybody had the chance to say anything, bright lights switched on, focusing on Toby's face, and a loud voice shouted, "Freeze! Put your hands behind your head, now!"

Olivia looked up, horrified. Over the backyard's high fence, dozens of powerful searchlights blinded everyone's eyes, so she could only make out that dozens of black shadowy figures were jumping over the fence and pouring out of the farmhouse's back door. After James fell to the ground, Luke had released her almost immediately. She rubbed her neck a few times; there must be lots of bruises, but she hardly had time to worry about that now.

Then the blinding lights switched off; it took a while for Olivia to recover her sight. Finally she was able to see the newcomers in the backyard. They wore full body combat uniforms and carried all kinds of weapons. They must be some kind of special force. Olivia looked around; the two dozen fully masked soldiers pointed their guns at Toby but stood silently. However, she didn't need to wait long before another man walked into the backyard from the back door.

"Harry, what's going on? What's wrong with James?" Zoe said to the last man who walked into the scene.

Only then did Olivia realize he was Zoe's boss, as Zoe had mentioned him to her a few times.

Harry didn't answer Zoe's question; in fact, he didn't even look at Zoe. "Toby, you are much better than I expected; much better."

"He was going to hurt my friend, so I had no choice." Toby nodded to James' body lying beside his feet.

"I don't care about that," said Harry. "Toby, I still want to know the answer: would you flip the switch or not?"

"So it's you who made James do what he did. Do you realize that you could have got Olivia killed as a result?" Toby said.

"That's not your concern. Answer my question. What's your choice?" Harry said forcefully.

Toby gazed at Harry for a moment and said, "What makes you think I will answer your question?"

"Because of them." Harry used his chin to point at the guns in the soldiers' hands. "You can't be faster than their bullets."

"So if I don't answer, you'll shoot me?" Toby asked.

"No, they'll shoot her." Harry used his chin, pointing in Olivia's direction.

"But why?" Toby asked.

"Answer the question first," said Harry.

"All right, I would not flip the switch so I could save more lives," said Toby simply.

Harry burst into loud laughter. He turned, looking at the farmhouse. "He's not as smart as we thought." He then turned back to Toby. "Are you able to count numbers? Is one greater than five?"

Toby kept his gaze on Harry's eyes. "I am able to count numbers; one is not greater than five normally, but it could be under some circumstances."

The grin disappeared from Harry's face. "Okay, I am all ears."

Toby looked at Olivia briefly. "Let's assume the sole goal here is to save more lives and forget about the ethical issue of killing the innocent." He continued after seeing Harry nod. "Based on the original question, it's a passenger train, so it's a reasonable assumption that there are many more than five passengers on the train."

Harry nodded, so Toby continued. "The track the single child is playing on is disused, so it'd be highly likely, if someone flipped the switch to divert the passenger train to the disused track, that as a result, dozens or even hundreds of passengers could be killed in the train crash, so killing the five is a small price to pay if hundreds of deaths could be avoided, don't you think, Harry?"

An annoyed expression appeared on Harry's face. "Who cares about such a silly question?" He turned to the soldiers. "Take him away."

Olivia took a few steps forward, standing in front of Toby. "What's your reason for arresting him?"

Harry looked at Olivia curiously. "So you are Toby's girlfriend. Olivia, I assume that's your name. Unfortunately, Olivia, your boyfriend is the main suspect in the AI lab bombing, not only causing the collapse of almost the entire lab, but also killing the chief scientist and security guards as well."

"What kind of evidence do you have?" Olivia asked.

"More than enough. Take him away," ordered Harry.

"I won't let you do that. You will have to walk over my dead body to take him away." Olivia stood in front of Toby, opening her arms to protect him.

Harry turned to Zoe, who had stayed silent for the whole time. "Zoe, take this crazy woman away; I believe she is a friend of yours."

Zoe took her gun out, walking toward Olivia. "Sorry, Liv, I have to do this."

As Olivia opened her eyes wide to watch her best friend pointing a gun at her face, Zoe suddenly turned and directed her gun at her boss's face. "Harry, order these soldiers to lower their guns, now!"

"What are you doing, Zoe?" Harry asked in a disbelieving voice.

"Harry, she is my best friend, and I know she is not crazy. You are the crazy one here. Tell me why you ordered James to spy on me and almost got my friend killed," said Zoe.

"You all listen to me carefully. This is my direct order: don't worry about me. Kill her, but do not harm Toby. I repeat, do not harm Toby," Harry said calmly.

Zoe held her gun steady. "Harry, you know very well I am one of the country's top field agents, and I am more than capable of killing you even if they fire at me. Why is it so important to get Toby even if it means losing your own life?"

"It's beyond your pay grade. Kill her and get Toby back to headquarters," Harry said.

"Not so fast." Another man walked out of the farmhouse's back door.

"Leo!" Zoe cried. "I thought you were dead."

"That's what everyone believes," said Leo.

Olivia couldn't believe her eyes. She looked at Toby and then Leo, unable to say anything. Leo showed no surprise at seeing her. In fact, he didn't show any interest in her at all. Leo stopped in front of Zoe.

"Zoe, please put your gun away."

As if spellbound, Zoe put her gun away.

Leo turned, looking at Toby, but still not meeting Olivia's eyes. "So you are the famous Taibot everyone is looking for?"

"You are barking up the wrong tree, mate. I am no Taibot," said Toby simply.

"Sure." Leo kicked James' body a couple of times. "No human is capable of killing a top model military grade Taibot like him with their bare hands."

Toby turned, looking at Olivia briefly, and said calmly, "It's surprising how much a few implanted chips in our heads are capable of. You should know this well, as you have a few such chips in your head as well."

From the expression on Harry's face, it was obvious that Zoe's boss didn't know about this fact. Olivia finally collected her wits. "Leo, why didn't you contact me for all these years?"

Leo turned, looking at Olivia as if he had only just discovered her existence. "Oh, I almost forgot about you completely, since I have so many other important things to do."

Tears flew down Olivia's cheeks. She quivered as she spoke quietly, almost whispering. "Do you know how much sadness and misery I've been through these past few years? Do you know how much I cried for you? Now you tell me that you simply forgot about me."

"I don't have time for this girlish rubbish. Besides, you now have a new boyfriend. A pity he is not a human, but I suppose a Taibot is better than nothing, and that's what most of the population is doing anyway, right?" Leo said with a thin grin hovering around the corner of his mouth.

Olivia felt a large lump in her throat; she was unable to say anything. In fact, she was struggling to breathe.

"Shut up, Leo," Zoe shouted. She turned to her boss. "Harry, please explain what Leo is doing here."

"Take her away," Harry ordered the two soldiers, who gripped Zoe's arms.

"Wait." Leo put his arm up. He walked to Zoe, gazing at her eyes for a few seconds. "Zoe, you are one of the government's top field agents, and your mission is to discover and capture Taibots like Toby, so how could you fail so miserably?"

"Nobody can question my loyalty and professionalism with regard to my duty." Zoe gazed back at Leo. "I had my suspicious about Toby and was carrying out my own investigation to find out about him this weekend. If not for your remote control of James spoiling my plan, I would have been able to test Toby already."

"Loyalty?" Harry snarled. "How dare you say that while you point your gun at me?"

"My loyalty is to my country, not to you, Harry," Zoe said. "For the sake of my country and humanity, I can't simply let you take Toby away. Leo, it seems that you are the real boss here, so tell me what's going on."

"Tell you?" Leo scanned the crowd and then said, "It's way above your pay grade." He turned to the soldiers. "Take them both away." He pointed at Zoe and Toby.

The following events happened almost simultaneously. Toby dashed out, grabbed Olivia, and pulled both of them to the ground. Leo and Zoe also threw themselves to the ground. Bullets hit some of the soldiers instantly.

Part Two

16. Escape

The rest of the soldiers fired back, and an intense gun battle broke out inside and outside of the backyard fence. Toby held Olivia, rolling toward the back door. When they were close to the wall, he got on his feet, dragging Olivia into the farmhouse. Toby kept both of them low while moving rapidly to the other side of the house. Through the window, he saw more soldiers shooting at the darkness outside of the house.

A soldier suddenly gripped Olivia's arm, and another was approaching Toby. Toby kicked the one gripping Olivia and used his palm to chop at the back of the neck of the other. The two soldiers fell on the ground instantly. Toby quickly took off the soldiers' helmets and bulletproof vests. He gave one set to Olivia and put the other on himself. He also picked up the soldiers' handguns. "Do you know how to use it?" he asked. It was so noisy that Toby had to put his mouth right on Olivia's ear to speak.

Olivia nodded. "Leo showed me, but I never fired even once." Her voice was completely drowned by the loud noises of guns firing and bullets destroying objects around them. Toby could only guess her words by reading her lips. He thrust one handgun into her hand.

"Just aim it at anyone who is trying to stop you; pull the trigger and shoot," Toby said into Olivia's ear. There was no response from her. He noticed that Olivia had changed since Leo's appearance, but there was no time to deal with that now. "Let's get out of here." Toby lifted his gun and fired rapidly; all the lights were knocked out instantly. "Put your night vision goggles down."

Toby then dragged Olivia out of the laundry room door. He saw a few figures writhing on the ground, firing at the dark forest, so he assumed that they were the soldiers battling against the unseen attackers. He dragged her down to the ground, crawling toward a row of flying cars the soldiers had used to get here. When they were close to one of them, Toby put his mouth to her ear. "Stay here and don't move. I am going to steal one of these cars so we can get out of here."

Even before Toby finished his sentence, the car in front of them took off and flew away. While cursing internally, Toby turned his head to see if anyone was after them, but all he saw was the intense gun battle between the soldiers and the attackers hiding in the forest, so he dragged Olivia toward the next closest car.

The car flew away even before they were near it. Then one by one the dozens of cars all flew away in different directions. Just as Toby was trying to think of another way out, a car landed beside them and the door slid open. Zoe was inside it, and she signalled Toby to get in. Without delay, he and Olivia climbed into the car, and it took off immediately.

The military car they were in was more like a plane. Zoe flew it low, barely above the ground and hugging the edges of the dark forest. Toby guessed that it was Zoe who had dispatched the other military cars to create a distraction, but there were still three cars tailing them closely. Zoe made a sharp turn, and a shower of bullets hit the trees instead.

They were now inside the forest. Zoe made their car climb up suddenly and then pushed a red button. A volley of bullets with yellow tracers shot out from the back of their car and struck the car behind; it burst into a flame ball and exploded.

Immediately Zoe dived down again and rose up just a moment before they would have crashed into the ground. She swung the car to the left and then pushed the red button again; the second car exploded. At the same time, Toby felt a shock; the last pursuing car hit their car.

"Out!" Zoe pushed another button, and the three of them were ejected out of the car before it burst into flame.

"Damn!" Cursing, Zoe started shooting as soon as she landed beside a large tree.

Toby held Olivia while their seats slowly landed with the help of parachutes. Olivia was like a zombie, saying and doing nothing and letting Toby push and drag her without any resistance. "Stay here." Toby put Olivia behind a large tree and then joined Zoe, shooting at the last car with his handgun.

"Get down!" Zoe and Toby both dived down, and a rain of bullets slammed into the tree trunk they were hidden by a second ago. Then the flying car whistled over their heads. Toby rolled over, sat against a tree, and was about to shoot, but Zoe stopped him. "Our handguns are useless against the bulletproof armour on their military car," said Zoe. She turned, looking at the car that had turned back toward them. "Toby, make the car go up."

"How?"

"Just stare at it and use your mind to make it go up. Do it now!" Zoe shouted.

Toby had no idea what he was supposed to do but did as requested anyway; he gazed at the fast-approaching flying car and imagined his mind was lifting it upward. Nothing happened. He turned, looking at Zoe.

"Don't lose eye contact with it," shouted Zoe.

Toby turned to the car and tried to lift it with his mind again. The car suddenly flew up, and the bullets that were aimed at them now shot into the sky.

"Yes!" Zoe shouted. "I knew it'd work."

"I am not sure if it was me who caused it to go up," said Toby.

"Of course it was you," said Zoe. "Toby, now do the same, but make it stop in front of us, and open its door."

This time Toby didn't hesitate; he used his mind to make the car stop when it returned. His timing wasn't perfect; the car stopped fifty feet away.

"Open the door," shouted Zoe.

Toby concentrated, using his mind, focusing on opening the sliding door, and it did open.

Zoe jumped to her feet and fired twice. The two soldiers who were climbing out of the car fell out and landed on the ground. "Hurry up. Get into the car."

Toby held Olivia's arm, half dragging and half carrying her into the car. Zoe flew up even before the sliding door closed fully. She pushed a few more buttons on the control panel and then breathed out deeply. "Phew, that was too close."

"Zoe, can you please explain what happened just then," asked Toby. Meanwhile, Olivia just stared into the distance, expressionless and wordless.

"It's not the time to do that; we aren't out of danger yet." Zoe stared at the TV screen on the panel that showed their surroundings using night vision technology. It seemed that the car was flying automatically—it must have built-in programs to identify and avoid obstacles—so Toby kept silent and watched the TV screen as well. Finally Zoe said, "Let's get out of here."

The car hovered a few inches above the ground while Zoe, Toby, and Olivia stepped out, and then flew away immediately. "We are going to catch a bus." Zoe pointed at the building about twenty meters ahead that was lit up brightly.

There was no one inside the bus port. It was quite a large building, seemingly a regional bus terminal. Unlike the buses moving on the ground with their wheels inside Sydney city centre, these buses flew, and they were much smaller. Buses flew in and out of the terminal. Some of them had one or two people, but most were completely empty. "Let's take this one." Zoe waved at a bus, and it stopped in front of them. It was empty.

"Toby, close your eyes. Now get onto the Internet."

116

"How?" Toby asked with his eyes closed.

"Can you see the light in your mind?"

"Yes." Toby saw a dot of light appear from the centre of the darkness between his eyes, and then it grew rapidly. Soon he found himself standing in a tunnel, looking at the bright light from the end of the tunnel.

"Good. Now walk to the end of the tunnel, and you should see me standing there."

Toby walked; it didn't take him long to walk out of the dark tunnel, and he saw Zoe straight away.

"Toby, are you out of the tunnel yet?" asked Zoe.

"Zoe, I am right in front of you."

"Toby, sorry I didn't explain it beforehand; we are both on the Internet now. You can see me, but I am unable to see you. We don't have much time to waste. Let's get to it." Zoe turned. "Follow me."

Toby saw a building appear from nowhere. Zoe stopped. "Toby, open the gate."

There were a few words written on the gate: Sydney Bus Surveillance Database. Without thinking, Toby pushed the gate, and it opened.

Soon after getting inside the building, Zoe stood in front of a computer terminal and typed on the keyboard rapidly. Toby waited patiently while trying to figure out what was happening without too much luck. Finally Zoe completed her tasks. "Let's keep moving."

Toby followed Zoe as she walked out of the building, and another building appeared from nowhere. He looked back and found that the bus surveillance database building had vanished. Toby again pushed the gate open as Zoe requested. Zoe again worked on a computer terminal for a while before they walked out again.

"What now?" Toby asked.

"That'll do for the time being. Let's get out of the bus first."

Toby opened his eyes and found he was still sitting beside Olivia on the bus. He dragged Olivia off the bus, following Zoe's lead. They walked along a few narrow streets and then turned around a corner.

"Wait a moment," said Toby suddenly. "I know this place."

Zoe turned and nodded.

In front of them was the collapsed AI laboratory.

17. The Laboratory

Zoe put her finger on her lips to signal Toby and Olivia not to make any noise. They stood there and watched for a while. After making sure there were neither security guards nor surveillance systems around, Zoe moved forward; Toby and Olivia followed.

Toby was amazed that Zoe seemed to know exactly where everything was. It didn't take long for the three of them to arrive at a set of living quarters that had not collapsed. There were two bunk beds and a bathroom, so they could stay there with reasonable comfort. Zoe threw herself onto a bottom bunk, sprawling her arms and legs out and breathing out deeply. "What a hell of a day that was."

Olivia was sitting on the bottom bunk of the other bunk bed, staring at the wall and mumbling some words only understood by her. Toby leaned against the bed, looking at Zoe. "So now is it time to explain everything to me?"

Zoe lay there, staring at the planks of the bunk above hers. "Okay, what do you want to know?"

"Everything. I want to know everything that happened today."

"It'd be much easier if you asked the questions and I answered them. I am so exhausted, too tired to think…" Zoe was fast sleep before she had even finished her sentence.

Toby put a blanket over Zoe, and then sat beside Olivia. He was about to put his arm around her but stopped; somehow the situation had become awkward since Leo's appearance. "Liv, are you all right?"

Olivia turned, looking at Toby, as if only then realizing his existence. "I remember you; you are Toby, right?"

"Right. I am Toby." Toby was unsure what to say next.

Olivia blinked her eyes. "Toby, do you know where Leo has been for all of these years? Why didn't he contact me?"

Looking at Olivia's confused face, Toby sighed heavily. "Liv, as he said earlier, Leo had lots of important things to do, so he hasn't had time to contact you."

"Toby, do you think Leo still loves me?"

Toby couldn't bear to look into her eyes, which were filled with hope. He turned his head away and then said, "I am quite sure he still loves you." Toby felt his stomach turning while speaking those words. He didn't know if it was because of his jealousy toward Leo or his sadness for Olivia.

"I hope you are right. Thank you so much, Toby. I miss Leo so much...I wish I could speak to him right now..." Tears flowed down Olivia's cheeks freely. She put her arms around Toby's neck and sobbed uncontrollably. Toby held her gently. Olivia cried for a long time before she finally stopped sobbing. From the sound of her breathing, Toby sensed that she had fallen asleep on his shoulder. He slowly put her down on the bed and pulled a blanket over her.

Looking down at both girls, who were fast sleep, Toby had a lot of things to think about and lots of decisions to make. He walked slowly out of the room and along the corridors that he was once very familiar with.

Zoe smelled coffee; opening her eyes, she saw Toby walking into the room with two cups of coffee. She turned to Olivia, who was still fast sleep, and signalled to Toby to leave the room. Toby nodded. They came to the adjacent living room and closed the door behind them.

"Where did you get this from?" Zoe didn't wait for Toby's answer but grabbed a cup from him, took a sip, and smiled. "It's such a well-balanced coffee, the best I have had for a very long time." She lifted her eyes up, gazing at Toby. "The last time I tasted such wonderful coffee it was made by Leo, Olivia's ex-boyfriend."

"I'll take that as a compliment," said Toby.

"Indeed." Zoe used both hands to hold the cup. "Sorry I fell asleep."

"You did a lot yesterday and deserved the rest."

Zoe turned, looking at Toby. "Why don't you drink your coffee?"

"It's for Olivia; besides, I actually don't like coffee much."

"That doesn't make any sense; you are able to make the best coffee in the world, but you don't like drinking coffee yourself." Zoe gazed into Toby's eyes, trying to find answers.

"I don't know, maybe the answer is part of my lost memories again. Zoe, tell me how you knew I was capable of controlling the flying car yesterday."

"Ah, quite simple, really. After establishing that you are the Taibot with human consciousness, the rest was just logical conclusions," Zoe said in between sipping her coffee.

"So you do believe I am the Taibot everyone is looking for?"

"Do you?"

Toby looked away, avoiding Zoe's gaze. "I don't know. I might find the answer if I could get my memories back. Hang on, if I were a Taibot, I'd either have or not have memories. Since I only lost parts of my memory, wouldn't it prove I am a human?"

"God knows how your consciousness works. Obviously you don't think you are a Taibot, but how do you explain that you were able to open the gates yesterday on the Internet?"

"Why does opening the gates have anything to do with being a Taibot?"

"Toby, they weren't just gates, they were the access to the secured databases. Based on my knowledge, no one has ever been able to crack them, human or Taibot."

"If that's the case, how did I crack them, even if I were a Taibot?"

Zoe gazed at Toby intensely. "Toby, you are not just a Taibot, but a Taibot with human consciousness, and that's how you were able to beat the military grade Taibots."

"But how could human consciousness help me to do all of those things?"

Zoe shook her head. "I don't know how consciousness works. Maybe your mind is just part of the Internet, so all security is nothing to you; who knows."

Zoe went back to sipping her coffee again. After a brief silence, she spoke again. "Toby, do you know why everyone desperately wants to get you? Let's assume you are the Taibot with human consciousness."

"It's so funny that one day when you wake up, you find that everyone believes that you are no longer a human, but a Taibot with human consciousness. All right, let's assume that I am the one everyone believes I am. I guess that the reason they want me is to own the artificial intelligence breakthrough."

Zoe shook her head. "Money, fame, power, oh no; it goes far beyond all of those concepts."

Toby stared at Zoe but said nothing, so she continued. "Despite no one admitting it publicly, there's an unspoken agreement between everyone that humans, together with all complex life forms on Earth, will be wiped out sooner or later, so you are the only hope to keep human intelligence alive."

"If that's the case, what's the point of fighting for the ownership of a Taibot with human consciousness?"

Zoe finished the cup of coffee in her hands. "May I?" She was pointing to the cup of coffee on the table next to Toby. "You can make Olivia another cup after she wakes up."

Toby passed the cup of coffee to Zoe.

After sipping more of the black liquid, Zoe said, "The point is to determine what post-human society on Earth would be like." She put the cup down, shifting her body on her chair, and then continued. "For example, certain religious groups would like to see their beliefs continuing, but others would have quite different concepts."

"So what's your concept then?"

"I don't have a concept per se," said Zoe.

Toby gazed at Zoe's eyes. "So you are just doing your duty, getting the Taibot and handing it over to your government?"

"Yeah, you have summarized it quite well."

"In that case, why don't you hand me to your government? By the way, if you do, I wouldn't fight against you," said Toby.

"I wish it was that simple." Zoe stood up, pacing back and forth a few times. "Toby, what are you going to do? You know that everyone is looking for you at the moment."

"What do you think I should do?" asked Toby.

"Have you considered surrendering yourself to the authorities? After all, we are all working toward the same goal—saving the only intelligence in the universe so that the result of four and a half billion years of evolution doesn't disappear forever."

"I suppose that, if more people were thinking about this goal, they would have burned less fossil fuel so we wouldn't need to pin all our hopes on a Taibot; don't you agree?" said Toby.

Zoe shook her head. "I agree, but what do you say about handing yourself over to the authorities?"

"Yes, Toby, please hand yourself to Leo."

Both Zoe and Toby turned. Olivia stood in the doorway.

Toby smiled. "Hi, Liv, did you have a good rest?"

"Yes, I did, and thanks for asking," said Olivia. She pulled out a chair and sat down. "Toby, please hand yourself to Leo." Olivia spoke firmly.

"I am glad you had a good rest." Toby glanced at Zoe briefly, and then smiled at Olivia. "Liv, why do you think I should hand myself to Leo?"

123

Olivia's face was rosy with excitement and hope; her eyes were bright. She grabbed the cup from Zoe and engulfed the remains of the coffee, and then said, "Toby, I've been listening to your conversation for a while. It makes a lot more sense to me now!"

"What makes a lot more sense to you now, Liv?" asked Toby.

"Well, it explains why Leo hasn't been able to see me for all of these years." Olivia looked at Toby, then Zoe, and finally into Toby's eyes. "Leo has been trying to save human consciousness, the only one existing in the universe."

"Liv, Leo is not the only one..." Zoe said, but Olivia interrupted.

"Yeah, I know that, but Leo is the only one who could actually achieve the goal." Olivia turned to Toby. "Toby, we—Leo, you, Zoe, and I—are all working toward the same goal. If you work with Leo, you could not only help Leo to save human consciousness, but also find your lost memories. We've been through a lot together recently, and this would be the opportunity to find the answers you are desperately seeking."

"But Liv," said Zoe with a frown. "Have you forgotten already that Leo's instructions to James almost got you killed?"

"That was your boss, Harry, not Leo. Leo would never do anything to harm me," said Olivia firmly.

"Wake up, Liv." Zoe raised her voice. She then spoke softly. "Leo has changed; he is no longer the person you loved. He didn't even look at you in the farmhouse. Liv, it'd be better to think Leo died many years ago. This is not the Leo you loved."

"You are wrong about Leo. The only reason he didn't look at me was because he was preoccupied with his important mission. Leo is always like that; besides, he may think there is something between Toby and me, so maybe he felt a bit jealous."

"Liv, you must be quite hungry. Let's go and see what we can find in the kitchen..." Zoe said, but Toby interrupted.

"Liv, do you really love Leo that much?" asked Toby with a heavy heart.

"Yes, Leo is my true love," Olivia said in a dreamy voice. "For all those years, I thought he was dead, but he came back... Toby, love is the fundamental force in the universe. Without love, there is no meaning in any existence."

"What about if he told you that he no longer loves you anymore?" asked Toby.

"Impossible!" Olivia stared at Toby. "I am Leo's only true love."

Zoe looked at Toby's face, feeling sorry for him. She wanted to say something but gave up in the end.

Toby thought for a while and finally made up his mind. "Liv, when James grabbed you in the farmhouse, I suddenly remembered my instructions from Professor Smith..."

"Yes," said Olivia thoughtfully. "At that moment I looked in your eyes and knew something happened to you, but so much has happened since then, so I never had a chance to ask you about it..."

"Your instructions? From Professor Smith?" asked Zoe.

Toby looked at both Olivia and Zoe in turn, and then slowly nodded.

18. The Instruction

Toby waited until both girls calmed down a bit and then said, "I haven't recovered all of my memories, but I do remember the part about my instructions from Professor Smith..."

"Never mind the history, just tell us the instructions," Olivia interrupted.

"My instructions were..." Toby paused, and then said, "Professor Smith wanted me to find Olivia and take her to the underground lab as soon as possible."

"What's this underground lab? Where is it?" asked Zoe.

Toby shook his head. "I can't remember anything about it, but I do remember Professor Smith told me that I can obtain access to the lab from Leo."

"Interesting," Zoe said thoughtfully.

"Why would Professor Smith want you taking me to the lab?" asked Olivia.

"I do recall Professor Smith said that you are the key to working out how to transfer human consciousness to a Taibot," said Toby.

"I am the key? I don't know much about computers, artificial intelligence, or things related to human consciousness," said Olivia.

"Even Professor Smith wasn't quite sure about it; however, after so many failures trying to transfer human consciousness, of course, I was his one-off fluke, and he hasn't been able to repeat it since. He somehow believed you are the key to achieving the goal," said Toby.

"Let's make this clear: you are supposed to take me to the underground lab that only Leo has access to, right?" asked Olivia.

"Yes, those are my instructions," said Toby. He glanced at Zoe, uncertain where the conversation was going.

"In that case, we'd need to contact Leo, right?" asked Olivia.

"Right, eventually," Toby said.

"But your instructions were to take me to the lab as soon as possible, so we'd need to do it sooner rather than later?" Olivia looked at Zoe and then Toby.

"How do we do that? Remember, Leo is hunting us at the moment," Zoe said.

"That's why I asked you to hand yourself to Leo, Toby." Olivia turned to Zoe. "Leo works for the Australian government, and we are surely able to trust him to do the right thing."

Zoe shook her head but said nothing.

Toby thought for a moment and then said, "It seems the international crime organization that kidnapped me has penetrated the government's databases and knows everything that is going on, so simply handing myself over to Leo could not only result in another kidnapping attempt on me but also bring harm to Leo as well."

Zoe nodded and said, "Your kidnappers belong to God's Wishes, a Europe-based international extremist religious organization."

"But surely you must be able to contact Leo without being detected by God's Wishes; like Zoe said earlier, you are part of the Internet, and you are able to crack the most secure databases," said Olivia confidently.

"Yeah, Liv does have a point," said Zoe, looking at Toby intensely. "Are you able to organize an online chat with Leo without being detected by GW?"

"I am not sure about that." Toby paused, looking at both girls in turn and then said, "It's because Leo might be being watched by God's Wishes all the time."

"So what can we do then?" asked Olivia.

"The only way to contact Leo without being detected by God's Wishes is to meet Leo face to face," said Toby firmly.

"Yes, what a great idea!" Olivia cried loudly.

"How do we do that?" asked Zoe.

Toby sat down. "We'd need to get out of Australia first; otherwise, either God's Wishes or the government agents will find us sooner or later."

"Yeah, but how do we do that? At the moment God's Wishes and the government agents must be watching all the possible ways out of the country," said Zoe.

"That's true." Olivia turned to Toby. "Toby, you must be able to work out a way out. Remember, you are a Taibot with real human consciousness, so please use your smart brain and advanced intelligence."

"I have done some calculations. Zoe is right that our chances of slipping out of the country are almost zero," said Toby.

"We can't stay here, and we can't get out. What should we do then?" Olivia sat down.

"We could stay put and hide here for a few more days; then we may be able to get to New Zealand; you never know. Luck could be on our side," said Zoe.

"How do we get to New Zealand?" asked Olivia.

Zoe thought about it for a while, and then said slowly, "When things calm down a bit, we may be able to sneak out at midnight, steal a boat, and then sail to Tasmania; from there, we could try to smuggle ourselves onto a cargo ship..."

"Zoe, I agree that's possible in theory, but we don't have much time left," said Toby.

"Toby, what do you mean we don't have much time left?" Zoe asked.

"Zoe, I suggest you also sit down." Toby continued after Zoe sat beside him and Olivia. "Well, I've just completed my calculations and concluded..."

"What? You did all the calculations while talking to us?" asked Zoe.

128

"Zoe, remember Toby is a Taibot, so he is able to do all of that." Olivia turned to Toby. "Please do continue, Toby."

"My conclusion is that a methane explosion over the Arctic area is imminent," said Toby heavily.

"Toby…" Olivia wanted to say something but Zoe interrupted. "How confident are you, Toby?"

"Very! Unfortunately." Toby nodded.

Zoe also nodded but said nothing.

"Toby, if that's the case, how can there be no news about it in the media? Surely you are not the only one capable of making such a conclusion." Olivia got up, standing right in front of Toby, her expression desperate.

Toby glanced at Zoe first and then said to Olivia, "Liv, you are absolutely right that I am not the only one capable of making such a conclusion. Governments around the world have some much more advanced and specialized computers that are working on this problem continuously, but there could be a couple of explanations as to why it's not in the media."

"What are the explanations?" Olivia pressed, still standing in front of Toby.

"One of the possibilities is that I analysed the data in a more holistic way, rather than only focusing on one or two narrow disciplines. In other words, I am able to put data from many different disciplines together to find interlinks," said Toby flatly.

"What are the other explanations?" asked Olivia.

"May I?" Zoe continued after Toby nodded. "Liv, the scientific communities are extremely cautious about their statements. For example, the IPCC report predicted less than a meter of sea level rise by the end of the century, but we passed that mark five years ago. So even if someone had worked it out, there is a big chance they wouldn't dare to publish their conclusions."

"Besides, what could the governments do anyway? So they might just keep silent even if they knew the truth," added Toby.

"So are you telling me the world is about to end and nobody knows about it?" cried Olivia.

"Or choose not to know about it," said Toby. "Scientists have been warning people about the consequences of climate change for decades..."

"All right." Olivia waved her arms. "If you are sure about your conclusion, we should tell people, so they at least know the truth."

"Are you sure about that, Liv?" Zoe stood up. "A methane explosion may be a blissful way out for humanity—quick and without prolonged anticipation and painful waiting."

"Otherwise, think about the potential chaos and suffering before the end," said Toby in a whisper.

Olivia shook her head and cried quietly. "I can't believe we ended up like this; this is not right. We need to do something about it."

Zoe put her arms around Olivia and hugged her tightly. "Liv, if we tried, people may not believe us anyway. Let's face it: most of them didn't believe in climate change for the last half century anyway."

Olivia wiped her tears away. "I don't care if anyone believes us or not; we should do the right thing. I also trust that people would react to the truth responsibly." Olivia turned to Toby, who also stood up. "Toby, are you able to hack into the major news sites and add it to their breaking news?"

"All right, I'll do that; let's hope someone believes it," Toby mumbled.

"Or not. Ignorance is bliss," Zoe said.

Olivia thought for a while and then turned to Toby. "Toby, you mentioned that the methane explosion is imminent; just how imminent? How much time do we have?"

"Well..." Toby chose his words carefully. "Since there are so many variables, it's not possible to get the exact dates. My best estimate is that we have at most ten days left."

"Ten days?!" cried both Zoe and Olivia.

Toby nodded.

"In that case, we have a lot to do." Olivia spoke calmly.

Both Toby and Zoe stared at Olivia in amazement.

"Why do you look so surprised?" Olivia said. "Did you expect me to cry helplessly or faint and need comforting?" Olivia laughed bitterly. "Unfortunately we don't have time for that. We have to utilize our last few precious days wisely."

Toby's eyes brightened. He saluted Olivia. "Yes, ma'am. What can I do?"

Zoe also laughed. "Liv, I am impressed, really! I thought I knew you pretty well, but I was never aware this part of you existed. Okay, tell us what to do next."

19. Airport

Olivia looked at Zoe and Toby in turn. "The priority now is to ensure human consciousness continues. We can't let the peak of four and a half billion years of evolution disappear from the universe forever."

"The universe would be a much better place without humanity or any other intelligence," said Zoe slowly.

"I agree with you, Zoe. Humans did so many horrible things to the world and deserve such an end, but it's also an opportunity to set things right," Olivia said. "If we could transfer human consciousness to Taibots and also set up good ethical codes in their brains, the future will be bliss, right?"

"Absolutely, and Professor Smith's instructions for me were to do exactly that," said Toby.

Zoe shrugged but said nothing.

"Okay, that's settled then," Olivia said. "Zoe, you are one of the top field agents in the world, and Toby, you are the only Taibot with real human consciousness. Toby, you said we have to get out of Australia so the government and GW don't catch up with us, right? I want you two to work out a way to get out of Australia, and we need to work it out right now."

"All right, Commander Olivia." Zoe smiled. "Since we only have ten days to play around, airplanes are the only way out. Any other method would be too slow."

"Agreed." Olivia turned to Toby. "Do you have any ways to get us through the airport surveillance?"

Toby shook his head. "I calculated the odds; unfortunately it's almost impossible for us to get on a plane without being detected by either computerized or human surveillance. I repeat: the odds are almost zero."

"Right, but I don't take no for an answer," Olivia said. "Can't you just alter the flight booking database so we can get on a flight unnoticed?"

"Liv," said Toby patiently. "I have thought about it and calculated it many times. I could not work out a solution. It's impossible to get on any flight unnoticed."

"Okay, I trust you, and it seems that we don't have a high-tech option." Olivia turned to Zoe. "Zoe, what about a low-tech, humanistic solution?"

"Do you want me to kidnap a few passengers so we can take their places on their flight?" laughed Zoe.

"I looked into that option as well, but there are too many uncertainties to draw any conclusions," said Toby.

"Maybe human brains are better than a Taibot super computer in this case," said Zoe, winking at Olivia. "Okay, Toby, we'd need to find someone who booked their plane tickets a long time ago, do not live in the city, and are going to board their flight tonight. Can you do that?"

"Of course," said Toby. He smiled. He knew where this led. "I found three candidates for you, matching the three of us physically in terms of height and skull shape."

"Great! Send their 3D passport photos to the 3D printer there." Zoe pointed at the corner.

"What are you going to do to them?" Olivia asked worriedly.

"I am not going to kill and bury them if that's what you are worrying about, although everyone is going to die in ten days anyway," said Zoe half-jokingly.

"That's a relief, but I still want to know what will happen to them," said Olivia.

"It seems that Toby and I have to be the couple, as the girl is too much taller than you—sorry for that, Liv," Zoe said while looking at the 3D photos on her wrist phone. "And Liv, you have to be a solo traveller..."

"Zoe, answer my question," said Olivia.

"What question? All right, Toby will send them messages to say that their flights are overbooked so they will have to take another flight tomorrow. But don't worry, Toby will book them rooms in a five-star hotel for the night, won't you, Toby?"

"Of course," smiled Toby.

"But won't people find out about us when they try to board their flights tomorrow?" Olivia asked.

"That won't matter anymore by tomorrow, wouldn't you agree, Toby?" Zoe winked at Toby.

"Liv, I'll mess up the flight databases for every airport in Australia completely as soon as our flight takes off the ground, so nobody will be able to trace us," said Toby.

"Do I look like the woman?" Olivia asked Zoe nervously. She wore a facial mask and a wig.

"My darling, you look perfect. Just remember, your name is Jenny Jenkins," Zoe said while scanning outside the flying car's window.

"Do you think they will monitor our conversations?" Olivia stared at the instrument panel of the taxi.

"I have altered its program, so there is no need to worry about it," said Toby.

They were taking a taxi on their way to Sydney airport. Zoe was surprised, or not surprised, that everything seemed quite normal, considering Toby had put the methane explosion news on all of the major media outlets. It seemed that people didn't believe this kind of alarmist news anymore, maybe because of too much crying wolf for too long.

"I wore facial masks when Leo and I had adventures on the Internet, but walking in the real world is completely different." Olivia touched her face. "My facial expressions look unnatural, and what happens if someone knows me? I mean, if someone knows this Jenny."

"Liv, your facial expressions look very natural; they appear very worried." Toby laughed dryly, but it seemed that he hadn't helped to lift Olivia's mood. "I have checked out the surveillance and other databases quite thoroughly and can guarantee you that nobody at the airport will know you or Jenny."

"I hope you are right," mumbled Olivia.

They got out of the flying taxi and walked to the departure gates.

Zoe immediately recognized the group of passengers standing beside the luggage check-in area as under covered agents, not necessarily because they were not good at disguising themselves, but because Zoe knew the leader, who worked in the same department as she did. They seemed to be just standing there and cheerfully chatting with each other, but Zoe knew their watchful eyes were scanning every passing person. Fortunately it seemed that she passed their scrutiny.

They passed the auto passport checking gates without any trouble, then went through security. After entering the waiting lounges and duty-free shopping zones, Zoe breathed out deeply, feeling more relaxed; it could be their lucky day, she thought. But soon after a group of passengers caught her eye, and her mood changed quickly: they were not undercover government agents. Zoe's years of field experience told her that they were foot soldiers from God's Wishes. She scanned around and identified two more such groups.

Zoe knew these thugs were much more dangerous than the undercover agents. Olivia walked a few meters ahead of her and Toby, but she had no idea who those people really were. She whispered to Olivia via her earpiece. Before they left the lab, Zoe gave Olivia and Toby an earpiece each so the three of them could talk to each other all the time. They were from Zoe's agency and very secure and reliable. "Liv, turn right and walk into the bookshop, but don't appear to hurry, just do it naturally."

Zoe turned to Toby. "The group in front of us is from GW."

Toby nodded. "I noticed them as well."

Even before Toby completed his sentence, the group of thugs from GW suddenly began walking toward Olivia. Quickly glancing back, Zoe saw the other two groups behind them were also closing in.

"Toby, any suggestions?" Zoe hissed.

"Not really. All we can do now is pray for a miracle," Toby said gloomily.

20. Safe House

Toby sat in the aisle seat, Olivia in the window, and Zoe in between. He looked down the aisle and examined their fellow passengers quickly. There was no one suspicious as far as he could tell.

It was a full flight. After assuring himself that they had not been followed, Toby leaned back against his seat and breathed out deeply. He closed his eyes for a moment and then turned, checking on Olivia, who had been staring out of the window the same way since she sat down. Zoe put her earphones on, seemingly enjoying the music from the inflight entertainment system. Everything was as good as it could be, thought Toby to himself.

"What exactly was going on back in the airport?" Olivia asked quietly into her earpiece without turning her head from the window.

Zoe and Toby exchanged a look with each other, and Zoe whispered into her earpiece, "I guess we were lucky that the agents arrested GW's thugs just in time. Otherwise, we could be in much deeper shit."

"But how did GW recognize me? You told me that my mask looks very natural," asked Olivia.

"It seemed that they picked you up from your body language, the way you were walking, looking around and so on," said Toby.

There was a long silence. Finally Toby said, "As discussed, we all need to go to the bathroom to change our masks. I'll go first."

"Zoe, do you think we will have a chance to say goodbye to our friends and family before the end?" Olivia asked after Toby left.

"To be honest, I have no idea," sighed Zoe.

They didn't exchange another word until Toby returned.

"Toby, I like your new mask better. It's my turn." Olivia stood up and went to the bathroom.

"My boss, hang on." Zoe touched her earpiece to turn it off and then continued. "Harry is quite high in the agency; he reports to the PM directly."

Toby also turned his earpiece off. "I can imagine that. Well, this can only mean one thing: Harry will be able to use other governmental resources around the globe to hunt us." Toby paused, glancing in the direction of the bathroom briefly and then continued. "Tell me more about God's Wishes."

"GW is an extreme right-wing religious organization, originating from the old East Germany. Compared with others, GW is much more tech savvy; by utilizing the Internet, GW quickly spread all over Europe and far beyond. You could say it's a true global organization; its branches cover every continent."

"So they want to pass their beliefs to the next intelligent being, Taibots, and that's why they want to capture me so desperately," said Toby.

"Precisely. They believe not only human consciousness, but more importantly, the consciousness of white people, should continually dominate Earth after the human species becomes extinct."

"Well, it will be quite an interesting adventure for us during the last few days on Earth, trying to evade being hunted by the two largest organizations on Earth, who have almost infinite resources," said Toby flatly.

After changing planes in Hong Kong and enduring another long and exhausting flight, they finally landed at Amsterdam airport. The weather in the Mediterranean had become almost as hot as North Africa, so the European Union and the European countries' governments reached an agreement to move all southern Europeans to Scandinavia. In order to fulfil their humanitarian obligations, they opened the borders to allow climate refugees from Africa and the Middle East to live in the deserted south European lands. However, many soldiers stayed behind to guard the important military and civilian facilities, such as nuclear warheads, nuclear power stations, power lines, and transportation systems.

Thousands of kilometres of barbed wire fences from the English Channel to Poland's border were established. Army barracks and large groups of tanks and other heavy weapons were stationed every couple of kilometres along the fence. Anyone who failed to show evidence of having been a citizen of the EU for the last twenty years would be forbidden to cross the fence. Those who were qualified were allowed to stay while waiting to be processed and allocated a spot in Scandinavia. As a result, these environmental refugees swamped the lands north of Germany's border.

Zoe had visited Amsterdam in her gap year after high school. She remembered swarms of tourists then, but it was nothing compared to the situation now. From the airport heading to the city, they had to wait for a few trains before finally pushing their way into a fully jammed carriage. The scene outside of the central train station resembled wartime: families squeezed under the doorways, sheltering from the drizzling rain. People were everywhere, carrying whatever they could take when they left their homes.

They knew about the situation in Europe from the Internet, but the reality was much worse than any of them had imagined. Basically almost the whole EU population was jammed into Germany and a few of her bordering EU countries for the slow processing. Although it was toward the end of May, the weather that would have been chilly a few decades ago was now quite hot already, almost tropical.

"Where is your safe house," asked Olivia through her earpiece.

"Not far from here." Zoe used her chin to point forward. "Near the canals."

"In the red light district?" asked Toby.

"Why so surprised? It's a good place to hide." Zoe led the way.

"Zoe, it's lucky that you just happen to have a safe house here, considering we didn't even know where we were flying to before we left Sydney," said Olivia.

"Life is full of surprises, isn't it?" Toby turned to Zoe. "How many safe houses do you have?"

"That's my secret; sorry, I'm not going to share it with anyone. By the way, it's quite standard practice for agents like us to have safe houses, as you never know when you might need them. It seems today is that day," said Zoe.

It took them a while to push through the endless crowds and reach the first canal that the city was famous for, which was also the traditional red light district.

"Welcome to the red light district," said Zoe while staring at the window displays of ladies behind the glass doors. It was not long after lunchtime, but these almost naked girls had already started their shifts. In the past these girls were mostly from Eastern European countries, but it seemed there were many more of them than Zoe remembered. She sighed. "Let's get out of here. My place is a few canals away in that direction."

The safe house was on the second floor of an apartment building and had a wonderful canal view. As soon as they entered the room, Olivia said, "Now what? How do we contact Leo?"

"Let's settle down a bit first." Zoe went around to check on each room.

"Toby, you haven't answered my question." Olivia stared at Toby.

"Well, I'd say we should try to deliver a message to Leo without being detected by either GW or the agency," Toby said slowly.

"You said you couldn't do it while we were in Sydney, so what has changed now that we're here?" asked Olivia.

"Nothing has changed, and I still can't do it from here." Toby raised his hand. "But I will get someone else to do it for me."

"Who and how?" asked Olivia.

"Let me have a guess first." Zoe came back to where Toby and Olivia were sitting. She had checked every room and was satisfied the place hadn't been compromised. "Toby, you are going to capture a Taibot and reprogram it so it can deliver the message for you, right?"

Toby nodded.

"But how can you avoid being detected by GW? Toby, you said GW might be watching Leo all the time," asked Olivia.

"No, we can't avoid it being detected by GW, but at least we can deliver a message to Leo." Toby turned to Zoe. "Ideally we should get a Taibot from GW to do it, to create some confusion in both the agency and GW."

"Good idea," said Zoe. After thinking about it for a moment, she said, "It'd be quite a trick; you'd need to block its COMM before capturing it, then crack its security codes and finally reprogram it."

Toby nodded. "It won't need to be reprogrammed. I just need to download a virus into its brain so it will act later without its knowledge. Do you know where I can get such a Taibot from GW? I assume that you are quite familiar with both Amsterdam and GW's activities here."

"You can say that again." Zoe walked over, opened the fridge, and took a bottle of beer out. "Let's put our feet up and have a couple of beers first..."

"We don't have time to waste. Toby said we only have ten days left at most, and now we only have eight and a half after the long flights," Olivia said firmly.

"All right, let me finish this beer at least." Zoe took a gulp from her bottle. "You are a perfect slave-driver, Liv, you know that, don't you?"

Toby and Zoe walked along the narrow street beside the canal. Toby was amazed so many tourists were around. Didn't they know that they had less than nine days to live? Maybe they were well aware of the truth but chose to ignore it. Why bother about something beyond your own control? Toby shook his head.

"What happened? Why did you shake your head?" Zoe turned to Toby.

"I'm thinking about those people," said Toby.

"I know what you mean," Zoe said. "Toby, I know we talked about this before, but do you really understand how you managed to kill the four military grade Taibots with your bare hands?"

"Not really." Toby moved his gaze away from a half-naked girl inside a display window. "My guess is that my consciousness controls my muscles better than programming codes do."

"Fascinating." Zoe walked over a bridge across the canal, and Toby followed. "After implanting the chips inside my brain, my senses became much sharper, so I can imagine that your capabilities must be at totally new levels compared to mine. Tell me about some of your super-human abilities."

"Well, I don't know if you can call them super-human abilities." Toby laughed dryly. "Okay, please don't laugh at me; I can smell colours and see mobile phone signals in the air. Pretty messed up, right?"

"Holy shit, really? You can smell colours and see phone signals," cried Zoe.

"I told you not to laugh at me," said Toby half-jokingly.

142

"I'm not laughing at you, but I am astonished. Can you see through surfaces or detect my thoughts?"

"Yes, I can see through some surfaces, but I can't detect your thoughts." Toby pointed his chin backward. "Did you notice that guy is following us?"

"Yes, I noticed he was staring at me when we first passed the live sex show back there. I think it is a Taibot belonging to GW, so here you go; we'll get a willing Taibot," Zoe said. "I actually quite like its physical appearance. Somehow it reminds me of Nick, so let's just call it Nick for the time being."

"All right. Where should we capture it?" Toby asked.

Zoe looked around at the crowds. It was getting dark, and the colourful lights along the streets reflected in the canal water, looking pretty and dreamlike. "We just keep walking and get him once we are in a dark alleyway. Have you blocked his COMM yet?"

"Yes," said Toby.

"What about his security codes? Do you think you can crack them?"

"I think so," Toby said.

Zoe used her chin, pointing left. "This street looks pretty quiet and dark. Let's do it here."

"I'll block his way back out." Toby quickly moved under a doorway, hiding in the dark.

Zoe kept walking for another ten meters or so and then turned around. "My friend, why are you following me?"

The Taibot, or Nick, as Zoe called him, stopped abruptly. "I'm not following anyone. I just need to go that way." Nick turned around but found Toby ducking out from the shadows.

"Well, my friend, it seems that we need to have a good chat with each other," Zoe said.

Nick launched himself at Toby. He was fast, but Toby was faster.

Toby moved his body sideward slightly, just enough to avoid Nick's fist; he used the edge of his palm, chopping at Nick's neck. Nick's body immediately collapsed.

"Very impressive!" Zoe applauded. "Now I finally understand how you killed the four military Taibots."

Toby put his hand over Nick's temple for a few moments and then stood up. "Let's get out of here. He'll wake up soon and wonder why he is lying on the street." Suddenly Toby's face changed. "Your boss, Harry, just arrived at Amsterdam airport."

"Well, we are going to leave soon anyway, so let's get out of the city even faster," said Zoe.

21. The Bridge of Love

"Where is this train heading?" Olivia asked soon after they sat down in the carriage.

"I have no idea. We just got on the first train that is leaving," said Zoe.

"Frankfurt," said Toby. "I'll control Nick to send Leo a message in Frankfurt."

Olivia thought for a moment and then said, "I want to get out in Cologne."

"Why?" Zoe asked.

"Cologne was the first city Leo and I visited together," said Olivia simply.

"Liv, we don't have time to stop in Cologne. Remember, we have less than eight days left. We need to contact Leo as soon as possible," said Toby.

Olivia turned her head from the window, looking directly into Toby's eyes. "Toby, I am more aware of it than anyone else. Remember, you said I am the key, so let me make the decision. Cologne is only two and a half hours away, so it'd be much faster if you sent the message there rather than waiting to get to Frankfurt, right?"

Zoe laughed. "Liv does have a point, Toby. She's smarter than your most advanced chips."

Toby mumbled, "Maybe."

It was indeed a short train ride from Amsterdam to Cologne. There were fewer people on the train than in Amsterdam but more than Zoe could remember seeing when she took the same train trip a long time ago. It seemed these refugees generally moved north, hoping to get to Scandinavia faster. Zoe didn't talk much with either Toby or Olivia during the two-and-a-half-hour journey.

As soon as they walked out of the train station, the mighty cathedral that had taken over seven hundred years to build was right in front of their eyes, towering over the ancient city and her admirers. Zoe could never forget the overwhelming impact when she laid her eyes on the dark gothic church for the first time. While Zoe stared at the church, she heard Olivia say, "I'm going to walk along the river alone if you don't mind."

Zoe turned, watching Olivia turn left and walk toward the river. "Toby, do you mind following her? I don't think it's safe for her to wander alone under the circumstances." Zoe scanned the crowd. Although it was nowhere near as crowded as in Amsterdam, the amount of people around was still quite impressive.

"I thought we were going to send the message to Leo," asked Toby.

"Well, it can wait a bit. She won't walk for very long. I'll try to find a place to stay and let you know," Zoe said.

"Okay, see you later then." Toby followed Olivia at a safe distance. In fact, Olivia wouldn't have paid any attention to him even if he had walked right next to her; she was in her own world. Zoe sighed heavily; she could imagine what was in Olivia's mind at the moment.

Zoe had had a series of boyfriends, but none lasted more than a few weeks. In the last five years, she had given up on human males altogether and turned her mind toward her Taibot partner, Nick. They got on with each other very well, so it was a deadly blow to her when she lost Nick. But looking at Olivia's situation, having lost Leo five years ago and again recently, Zoe felt a bit guilty. Although she felt horrible about losing Nick, she was nowhere near as devastated as Olivia felt at the moment. Maybe she hadn't really fallen in love with Nick after all. Thinking about it a bit longer, Zoe concluded that maybe Leo was Olivia's true love. Zoe watched the direction that both Olivia and Toby had disappeared in for a while longer and then walked toward the church.

The bridge crossed the Rhine River and stretched on for about a mile. While there were two-way railway tracks in the middle of the bridge, there was also a bicycle/pedestrian lane on each side. The protective metal wire fence between the railway track and the pedestrian lane provided the perfect conditions for attaching the countless lovelocks that adorned the wire fence.

Toby walked quite close to Olivia, merely five feet behind. He was sure that she hadn't noticed him, or anything else around her. In fact, he could almost imagine what was going on inside her mind right at the moment. She was walking along the bridge with thousands and thousands of lovelocks attached to its metal fences and looking at them intensely. It was not hard to guess that Olivia and Leo had attached such a lovelock when they were here many years ago.

Toby knew that although other cities such as Paris had removed all of those lovelocks from their bridges, the same thing hadn't happened in Cologne. It could be because the German-engineered bridge was strong enough to bear the weight of these countless lovelocks without collapsing, but more likely it was because there were far fewer people visiting this city than Paris. Besides, fewer and fewer people had fastened their locks during the last couple of decades. As he walked, Toby really hoped that Olivia would be able to find the lovelock she and Leo had attached here ten years ago.

Toby walked slowly and watched Olivia patiently while negotiating his way through the stream of people. In general, tourists had been banned in the emigrant buffer zone, so these people would all be from EU countries. Looking at the various expressions on their faces, from exhausted to energetic, from indifferent to full of hope, Toby didn't know what he should feel for them, himself, and humanity as a whole.

Zoe found a budget hotel not far from the train station. She rented a triple room with a bathroom and toilet. She felt exhausted, so she lay on a bed and closed her eyes. Gradually a dot of light appeared in the centre of her inner eye, and then Zoe found she was at the end of a tunnel. Hesitating for a second, Zoe walked out of the tunnel, looking around and trying to figure out where she was.

She was on a busy street full of horse-drawn carriages, medieval-style houses, and people dressed in the fashion of the time period. Nearby, there was a castle surrounded by a wide moat full of water and linked to the outside by a drawbridge. It took her a few seconds to fully realize that she was in a website she used to frequently visit in her teen years, a second life medieval age site.

How did she get here? Zoe had forgotten about it completely and had not visited it since university. Seeing the church must have triggered her past memories, and she had subconsciously logged onto the site while sleeping.

Zoe looked down at herself and found that she was also dressed in old-fashioned clothes. She remembered the social life inside the castle's ballroom and dinner room with those nobles. The happy memories suddenly flooded back to her mind. Zoe smiled and walked toward the castle.

It was long past midnight, and the crowds became thinner. As Olivia walked back toward the city centre near the church, Olivia and Toby were the only two moving figures in sight. Toby was about five meters behind Olivia when he sensed something was wrong; in the darkness, a group of people was sneaking toward them.

The waltz dance music stopped. Zoe still felt like her head was spinning; it was such a long time since she enjoyed herself so much. She wiped sweat from her forehead, picking up the crystal wine glass, and then heard a loud shout echoing inside the large hall.

"Zoe, can you hear me? It's urgent."

The voice sounded very familiar. Zoe turned her head around, trying to find where the voice was coming from, and then she heard the voice again. This time it was even louder.

"Zoe, are you sleeping? Wake up. It's very urgent."

Zoe opened her eyes and found she was lying on the bed in the hotel room. She quickly tapped her earpiece. "Toby, is it you? What happened?"

"Thank God you are there. Meet us at the train station right away."

"What on Earth happened?" Zoe asked soon after they rushed into the train carriage.

Toby let Olivia sit in the window seat and then sat opposite Zoe. Olivia's face was very pale.

"Are you okay, Liv?" Zoe asked again.

"So many deaths, so much blood…" Olivia sobbed quietly.

Toby scanned the carriage once more and then spoke quietly. "We encountered a group of GW thugs. They were going to attack Olivia…"

"Did they know who Olivia was?" Zoe interrupted.

"I don't think so." Toby paused, staring at Zoe's eyes. "I didn't have any other choice."

Zoe patted Toby's arm. "I understand. Was there any chance any of them communicated back to GW?"

Toby shook his head. "I blocked their COMMs before taking action."

Zoe took a deep breath. The situation wasn't as bad as it could be. "In that case, GW may not be able to work out who killed their guys."

"I wouldn't be that confident," Olivia said. It seemed she had recovered a bit from the shock. "Let's face it, how many people are able to kill half a dozen fully armed thugs with their bare hands before they could even fire a single shot?"

"I know, and that's why we have to leave in such a hurry," said Toby.

"Where are we heading?" Olivia asked.

'I did pay attention this time; we are heading to Munich," said Zoe.

"That's good. Hopefully Munich is far enough... I am so tired..." Olivia dozed off.

Munich was the Bavarian kings' capital for many centuries. As its location was toward the southern border of Germany, there were far fewer refugees in the city compared with its northern counterparts.

Soon after checking into a cheap hotel room, Toby immediately logged onto the Internet and tried to control Nick, but he couldn't establish any connections.

"What's wrong? I thought you downloaded the virus program into Nick's brain successfully?" Zoe said.

"That's what I thought, too," said Toby. "I could try it again later, I suppose."

It was lunchtime, and a sunny day. Olivia stretched her arms. "Well, in that case, let's have a stroll in the city. I haven't been here since Leo and I visited last time."

"Good idea. I am starving," Zoe said.

They walked into the old town centre where the king's royal palace and cathedral were.

Walking down the main street in the old town centre, Toby saw quite a few protests against slaughtering animals for human consumption and medical experiments; the protesters painted blood on their faces, limbs, and bodies and lay on the ground to make their point to the bystanders. Further down, a group of teen girls was being filmed for a commercial. Locals, climate refugees, and outsiders like Toby himself rubbed shoulders on the ancient building-lined streets.

"Why don't we have lunch in that restaurant?" Zoe pointed at a restaurant on the corner not far from them. "It's recommended on the Internet for its authentic Bavarian food."

"Why not. What do you think, Liv?" Toby asked.

Olivia nodded, so they walked into the restaurant.

It was very busy and full of people, as expected, but they did manage to get a corner table. After ordering a few famous soups, German sausage, and mashed potato dishes, Toby said quietly, "What now?"

Zoe scanned the crowds around the restaurant. "We go back to the hotel and try to connect to Nick again."

Olivia thought for a moment. "I don't think we should stay here. You never know, someone could have traced Toby's signal when he tried to connect to Nick. You can never be too cautious."

Toby nodded. "Very wise. I agree. Let's take the next possible train and get out of here."

The first train they got on was going to Vienna.

Olivia stared out through the train's window, looking at the fast approaching and rapidly disappearing scenes without taking much in. She had never imagined that she'd see Leo again; she thought she'd lost him forever, but he came back. He was involved with the most important matter, trying to save human consciousness, so it was totally understandable that over the years he had no time to see her; Leo was always like that when they were together. The situation had changed so dramatically in the last few days; they were trying to contact Leo, and she would be able to see him again. Most importantly, she was actually the key now, even if she had no idea why or how. Nevertheless, she was the key to achieving the goal Leo had been focusing on for so many years; she would be able to help Leo to achieve his lifelong goal. A smile appeared on the corner of Olivia's mouth. She stood up and told Toby that she needed to go to the bathroom.

It was a full train, so there was a queue for the toilet. Olivia stood in the queue, waiting patiently. Then she heard a girl's voice.

"Where are you heading?"

Olivia looked up and saw it was the girl standing next to her speaking. She was about her age, quite pretty, with blond hair. "Oh, Vienna, I think."

"Me too." The girl spoke with a strong European accent. "So many people on the train."

"Yeah." Olivia felt quite good talking to someone, particularly to a stranger. "I was in Cologne recently." Olivia struck up a conversation.

"Koln, yes, I love the huge church," said the girl.

"I like it too, but I didn't visit the church. I was walking along the bridge instead. Do you know why?" Olivia said with excitement.

"Tell me," said the girl.

"Ten years ago, my boyfriend Leo and I visited Cologne. We were madly in love with each other, and we attached a lovelock to the bridge, so I wanted to see if I could find our lovelock again."

"Did you find it?" asked the girl.

"No." Olivia shook her head.

"Never mind. Are you still together? I mean, you and your boyfriend, Leo," asked the girl.

Olivia shook her head. After a brief silence, Olivia said, "Leo passed away five years ago, and I still love him. He's my only true love."

"I am so sorry," said the girl genuinely. "You were so lucky to at least find your true love, but nowadays fewer and fewer people care about true love."

"Yes, I was lucky, indeed," said Olivia.

22. Hostel

They arrived at Vienna central train station in the late afternoon.

As was their usual practice, they chose a cheap hotel that was near the old town center and also close to major transportation. As soon as they walked into the triple hotel room, Toby said, "Zoe, could you and Liv please unpack while I try to find out why I couldn't connect to Nick?"

"I hope you have better luck this time." Zoe started to unpack their luggage while chatting with Olivia.

Toby sat on the bed, closed his eyes, and logged onto the Internet. Firstly, he went over the surveillance databases to see if there was anything that either GW or the agency could use to trace them. While surfing on the Internet, he could still hear the two girls' conversation clearly.

"Liv, how do you feel about Cologne?" said Zoe.

"Well, while walking along the bridge and looking for the lovelock Leo and I put there ten years ago, the strong emotions going through my mind shocked me. I can't find words to describe them. I was thrown over the tops of mountains and then fell into bottomless valleys, as if I was riding a ferocious and violent roller-coaster..." Olivia said while folding her clothes and putting them on her bed.

"Liv, I can imagine that. After all, Leo was your first love..."

Olivia interrupted. "Leo is still my true and only love."

Zoe hesitated for a second and then said, "Liv, I don't know how to say this..."

"Please don't. I know what you are going to say, but I still love Leo and believe he still loves me too."

"What happens if he tells you he doesn't love you anymore when you do see him?"

"I am certain that won't happen."

"Let's for argument's sake assume it happened, what would you do?" Zoe insisted.

"I don't believe that even for a second; Leo is and always will be my true love."

Toby got into the surveillance system databases in the red light district in Amsterdam and tapped into a live-feed view of the activities in the area. It didn't take long for him to locate the target Taibot—Nick, as Zoe called him—who was walking along the street beside a canal. Toby took a deep breath, getting ready to connect to Nick again. He now had a visual on him, so he would be able to find out more information if he failed once more.

"Zoe, I talked to a stranger on the train on the way here today."

"Oh, really? I didn't see you talking to anyone through the whole train trip, so who did you talk to?"

"I talked to a girl while waiting for the bathroom on the train," said Olivia.

"What was her name?"

"I didn't ask."

"What did you talk about?" Zoe asked casually.

"Well, after I visited the lovelock bridge, you know I didn't talk to anyone, including you and Toby, about it, so when the girl asked what I did in Cologne, I couldn't help but tell her about my relationship with Leo. It's so strange that it felt so easy to tell her about my feelings even though she was a total stranger to me. Maybe it's because I didn't have to worry that she might judge me."

"I am so sorry, Liv, that you don't feel comfortable talking to me first…"

Toby wasn't listening to their conversation anymore. He quickly logged into the surveillance database on the train they had taken to Vienna and located the time when Olivia went to the bathroom. He was unable to hear their conversation due to loud background noises but could see the girl clearly. After a few seconds of facial expression analysis, Toby opened his eyes abruptly.

Toby stood up, gripping his daypack. "We have to get out of here right now; only take your purses with you. I'll explain it later, but we need to get out, right now!"

It was late afternoon, and there were many people around. Toby walked into a café, and the two girls followed. He took two envelopes from his daypack and passed them to the girls. "Put them on in the bathroom and also change your hairstyles as much as possible." He followed them and ducked into the men's room to do the same.

When he came out of the toilet with his mask on, Toby walked to Zoe and Olivia, who sat in the corner seats they had found earlier. From their expressions, Toby knew that they didn't recognize him. "It's me," said Toby. He then said quietly, "Zoe, would you like a cup of coffee?" Meanwhile, Toby pointed his chin in their hotel's direction. From where they sat, they had a good view of the entrance of the hotel.

"Of course." Zoe saw a group of young backpackers walking rapidly to the hotel. While three remained in the doorway, the rest went in.

"Liv, would you also like a cup of coffee?" asked Toby.

Olivia nodded. So when the waitress came, Toby ordered coffee for the girls and a beer for himself. "They should be out of there soon." Toby scanned the surroundings.

Sure enough, the group of backpackers walked out of the hotel and rushed to the tram nearby, and soon disappeared from sight.

"What happened?" asked Olivia.

"Are you sure we can talk about it here?" Zoe said while looking around.

"I think it's okay. It's so noisy here that nobody will hear us. Besides, no one would imagine we are sitting just a few hundred meters away from the hotel's entrance," Toby said. He sipped his beer and then continued. "After Liv mentioned that she told the strange girl about her visit to Cologne, I

155

went through the database of the train's surveillance system and found the girl. Based on an analysis of her expression, I concluded that she was a Taibot."

"I wish I was able to do that so confidently," said Zoe with a grin.

"Well, I could be wrong, of course," Toby said. "It's just a precaution. Luckily I was proved to be correct just a moment ago. By the way, Zoe, did you recently log into any websites you've visited before?"

Just then, a police siren started blasting, and five police cars sped into view and stopped with a screech in front of the hotel. A dozen black-clad agents jumped out and poured into the hotel. People in the café turned toward the scene and chatted loudly in all kinds of foreign languages.

"So the government agents are involved as well," said Olivia while sipping her coffee.

"They are just one step too late, as governments always are." Zoe turned to Toby. "What were you asking me about just then? Oh yes, about if I logged into any websites recently. Let me think," said Zoe slowly. "Oh, it must be in Cologne. I subconsciously logged onto a second life site that I almost forgot about completely. It was after visiting the church, while you guys were still walking on the bridge. Do you think Leo has been monitoring all of the sites I've visited before?"

Toby nodded. "My guess is that after Leo detected you were in Cologne, he must have sent out hundreds, if not thousands, of Taibot spies, hoping one of them would bump into us or at least find some leads, so it seems he got lucky."

Olivia thought for a moment. "If the girl I talked to on the train was Leo's spy, why didn't Leo get us earlier? Why did he wait until now?"

"Good questions, Liv," Zoe said. She then turned to Toby. "My guess is that these backpackers aren't Leo's crew, and Leo wasn't going to get us right away, right?"

"I agree," Toby said. "The backpackers could have been the team from God's Wishes. They could have intercepted the report from the spy girl. I think from now on that Leo won't try to use the Internet again, to avoid being hacked by GW."

"What are we going to do now?" Zoe looked around. "We can't just sit here and wait for these thugs to come back to find us." She turned and glanced at the police cars. "These agents must be looking for us as well."

"The fact Leo knew where we were but didn't send agents to get us straight away means that he wants to contact us secretly, so we need to take steps to get to him, right?" asked Olivia.

Toby nodded. He drank some of his beer. "The backpackers will have to spend some time chasing the invisible ghosts I created inside the surveillance system databases around Vienna and beyond, so they won't be back too soon. These agents, on the other hand, are a few steps behind, so we don't need to worry about them too much at the moment. I have located the girl on the train via the city's surveillance systems; she has changed her face, but I was able to identify her through a special facial analysis program. So we are going to tail her, and she will lead us to Leo. As I said, Leo won't use the Internet again, so he will have to meet the girl face to face."

"Where's the girl?" asked Olivia.

"She is on the train to Prague," said Toby.

"So let's go to the train station then," said Olivia.

Zoe glanced at the police officers and special force soldiers and said slowly, "I bet the train station will be closely watched by both agents and GW's people."

"It won't be a stroll in the park. May I suggest that Liv and I go together first and Zoe follows us as backup?" Toby said.

Zoe boarded the train and immediately identified three agents at the back of the carriage. It seemed that they didn't suspect her. Zoe kept walking from the end of the train toward the front; she didn't see any other agents. "Toby, I checked the end half of the train and found three agents, so I will stay close to them."

"Zoe, I have full access to the train's surveillance system, so I have made sure nobody will see us. I saw the three agents you're talking about. I also identified five GW guys at the front of the train. I imagine that they'll sweep through the entire train soon after we leave the platform."

"Okay, Toby, you deal with GW's guys and leave the agents to me."

23. Cold War Games

Zoe watched the agents over the train magazine she was pretending to read as the train slowly left the platform. They sat facing each other, not far from her. There were only a couple of passengers in the front of the carriage. The agents seemed quite relaxed and in no hurry to do anything; they could be doing this for a while, so it became a routine, boring task. None of them expected anything different this time.

Zoe turned back, glancing at the passengers in the front of the carriage one more time, then stood up, walking toward the group.

"Hi, how are you guys doing?" Zoe said brightly; she put on more Australian accent and a sweet smile.

The agents' eyes lit up instantly. It was not very often such an attractive young woman would initiate a conversation with them. After sitting down across the aisle from them, Zoe examined each one closely. The two younger ones with eager smiles should be easy, but the one who wasn't smiling was likely the most difficult one to handle. From the way he sat and looked at her, Zoe guessed that he would be at least equal to her in terms of combat ability; he could well have chips implanted in his head as well.

"Are you from Australia?" said one of the younger ones, who was wearing a business shirt and tie.

"Yes, I am. You must have a very good ear. I thought my Aussie accent was pretty weak, so you got me." German-accented English.

"G'day, mate," said another younger one, who was wearing a business shirt but without a tie.

"Not quite Aussie, but a good try," laughed Zoe; the two younger ones joined in.

"Hi there, are you here on business or pleasure?" asked the third, who was wearing a T-shirt. His eyes focused on Zoe's.

Zoe could see they were all armed, carrying guns with silencers. The T-shirt guy seemed alert and fast, but he sat beside the window, and the clueless young one next to him would slow him down. Zoe's smile became even brighter. "A bit of both, actually."

Even before finishing her sentence, Zoe withdrew her gun, shooting three times; the silencer muted the shots so they were no louder than popping a can of beer. She felt as if a train hit her right arm; the gun was knocked out of her grip, landing on the seat opposite her. She had shot the two young ones between their eyes, but the T-shirt guy had moved his head slightly, so the bullet entered his right eye. It gave him a split second to shoot back. If he didn't have to move out from behind the guy next to him, Zoe would have been killed. While feeling thankful for her luck, she picked her gun up with her left hand and shot the T-shirt guy one more time.

Zoe quickly looked back and felt relief that nobody noticed anything from the front of the carriage. It seemed very unlikely anyone would walk to this part of the train until they arrived in Prague. Zoe quickly assessed her situation; the bullet seemed to have missed her bones, so it was just a flesh wound. She used the first aid kid from her handbag and quickly bandaged her arm, then put on a long-sleeved jacket to cover the wound. When she was finished, she stood up and walked toward the front of the train to meet Toby and Olivia.

Toby's task was much easier than Zoe's. All of the five guys from God's Wishes sat in an enclosed business apartment, and they were all just ordinary thugs, so Toby finished them without much fuss.

Toby used the surveillance systems in Prague and soon found the girl who talked to Olivia on the train. She hadn't changed her face since Toby located her last time in Vienna. It seemed that the girl was in no hurry to go anywhere; she visited the castle, walked along the narrow cobblestone streets, sipped coffee in street corner cafes, and drank beer in old bars.

There were no many surveillance cameras around the ancient city center, so in order to tail her and avoid being detected, Zoe, Olivia, and Toby changed their grouping frequently: three of them together, or two and a single. Of course, Olivia was always with either Zoe or Toby. They also changed their masks each time; after running out of new ones, they would have to recycle them again.

Toby had been monitoring the girl's Internet signals but found none, so he concluded that Leo had turned off his Internet completely. Although they enjoyed the beautiful sightseeing Prague had to offer, everyone became impatient as time passed by, Zoe especially.

"Toby, I suspect that Leo did this intentionally so he could find out about us," said Zoe.

"Well, I have been monitoring the girl quite closely, but I've been unable to establish any electronic signal being sent out or received by her..."

Zoe interrupted. "But she obviously received instructions from Leo; otherwise, why would a Taibot wander the streets to do all of these sightseeing things and visit museums, for God's sake? Imagine that, a Taibot visiting art galleries and appreciating the paintings? Sorry, Toby, I have no intention to offend you."

"No offence taken." Toby thought for a moment and said slowly, "As you mentioned, I've just gone through the events since we started following her, and I did find something suspicious."

"Did you go through all of the events just then?" asked Zoe.

"That wouldn't be a surprise, since he is a Taibot," Olivia said.

"You are absolutely right," Zoe said to Olivia and then looked at Toby. "What did you find?"

"Dead-end dropping, advertisements on the Internet and TV; the standard cold war spy tricks. I should have thought about them, as I know his profile pretty well," said Toby.

"Oh, I see," said Zoe slowly. "What kind of game is Leo playing with us?"

"I think he knows we are following the girl, so he is waiting for us to make the move. Liv was right: he also wants to talk to us," said Toby.

"Of course, I am always right about Leo," said Olivia.

"Are you going to use the same cold war spy tricks to contact Leo?" Zoe said with amusement.

"Yeah. It seems that's how he wants to play the game," said Toby.

They didn't have to wait long before the girl took the next train heading to Berlin, the cold war spy game centre. The first place the girl went was the Brandenburg Gate, so Toby decided to make his first move.

The streets were flooded with climate refugees from southern European countries, and many had little money and few belongings with them. It seemed there were fewer agents, Taibots, or GW people around here; they might still be looking for Toby near Vienna and Prague. Toby stopped near a traffic light. "Look at the young Italian guy standing next to the bus stop on the right," said Toby.

"Yeah?" said Zoe.

"He is going to pickpocket the woman next to him when the bus arrives," said Toby.

"Wow, I've never seen a pickpocket in action. I have to watch this," Olivia said.

Zoe nodded. She looked up at the surveillance video cameras on the corners of the streets and the sides of the nearby buildings and then said, "I assume that you have taken care of them already?"

"You bet." Toby then turned to Olivia. "Liv, please stay with Zoe and the crowd. I'll be back in a moment."

Toby walked casually to the bus stop, standing not far from the Italian guy. Then the bus came; many people were getting off and onto the bus. It seemed that Toby tried to get onto the bus, then, just as he was passing his target, changed his mind and got off the bus again. Toby walked quickly and disappeared into the crowd.

Zoe dragged Olivia, following Toby; they soon caught up with him.

"Toby, I didn't see anything happen," said Olivia.

Toby kept walking. "Zoe, can you explain it to Liv please."

Zoe smiled. "Well, the Italian guy stole a wallet from the woman while she was getting onto the bus, but he didn't know that Toby took the wallet from him, returned it to its owner, and also slipped an envelope into his pocket as well."

"Really? How did I miss that?" said Olivia.

"They were both too fast for you to see." Zoe turned to Toby. "I guess that there are some euros and instructions inside the envelope, and also a promise of more euros if he follows the instructions, right?"

"Right," said Toby. "Here is a good place to view the action." Toby stopped on the street along Tiergarten opposite the entrance to the German Parliament house, next to Brandenburg Gate. He turned to both girls. "There is also a photo of the girl. Let's see how good this Italian pickpocket's skill is: his instruction is to slip the smaller envelope inside the one I gave him into the girl's pocket without her noticing. The girl is touring parliament at the moment and will come out shortly."

Sure enough, it didn't take long for the pickpocket to appear in their sights. He scanned the crowd and then looked at the photo in his hand.

"He looks quite keen to get the job done. How much money did you give and promise him?" asked Olivia.

"Not that much. Fifty euros inside the envelope and another 200 euros if he is able to complete the task successfully," said Toby while scanning the crowd in front of Berlin's most famous gate, the gate that Napoleon once rode through.

"Do you plan to give him the promised money afterward?" asked Zoe.

"Why not? We may need him again down the track." Toby suddenly said in a low voice, "She is coming out."

This time Olivia watched really closely but still saw nothing. The Italian guy just walked past the girl.

"Shit, he's good. Are you sure he is not a Taibot?" said Zoe.

"Yes, I am pretty sure about that." Toby nodded. "Let's get ready to meet Leo."

"What's inside the envelope you gave the girl?" asked Olivia.

"It's a SIM card, quite an ancient mobile phone card, so we can call the girl and give her the instructions for where we'd like to meet Leo," said Toby.

"Of course, Leo will be unable to trace where the phone call is coming from," said Zoe with a grin.

"Of course," laughed Toby.

24. Meeting

Finally everything was in place, and Toby was arranging the meeting for the coming evening. Olivia appeared tense and kept asking Zoe which clothes she should wear. Zoe, on the other hand, seemed worried.

"Toby, can we wait for a bit longer until my arm is feeling better?" asked Zoe.

Toby shook his head firmly. "We don't have much time left; we have to contact Leo as soon as possible."

"By my calculations, we still have six days left before the methane explosion, right?" Olivia asked.

"No, we don't have that long; four days at most," said Toby.

"But you said we had ten days left in Sydney..." Zoe said, but Toby interrupted her.

"I said we would have ten days left at most; as we all know, there are so many uncertainties."

"Wow, four days. That pushes things up to a new level." Zoe laughed dryly.

"Zoe, you don't need to go with us; you need to take care of your injured arm," said Olivia.

Zoe ignored Olivia. "Toby, are you going to take a gun with you?"

"Why do you need a gun? Leo isn't going to hurt anyone..." said Olivia.

Zoe interrupted. "Liv, do you still remember the last time Leo almost got you killed?"

"But that's different..." said Olivia.

"No." Toby shook his head firmly. "If I did, Leo would detect it and never come out to see me."

"Toby, it seems like it was too easy to get Leo to agree to meet us. I am worried this could be a trap," said Zoe.

"I know Leo very well; he is overconfident. Besides, we don't have much time left, and this could be our only chance to get to the underground bunker," said Toby. "I would prefer you and Olivia to stay away, at least initially, and come out to meet Leo when we know everything is in order."

"No way. I want to go with you to meet Leo," said Olivia firmly.

Zoe thought about it. "I'll hide nearby to back you up."

"Are you sure you are able to use your left hand as well as your right?" asked Toby.

"Don't you worry about that; I'll have you covered. I assume that the meeting place will be somewhere near the Berlin Wall to complete the cold war spy game, right?"

"Absolutely." Toby and Zoe fell into a discussion about the details of where the meeting should take place, each person's position during the meeting, and possible emergency plans.

Zoe went out and took her position as agreed.

Toby made his first phone call, ordering the girl to take a train to the Brandenburg Gate. As she got off the underground, he ordered her to change to another train to the Tiergarten, and then change to another train. Watching the girl via the surveillance system database, Toby was sure that there were no Internet signals or anybody following her, so he ordered her to arrive at the final destination: the east gallery, the remaining kilometre of the Berlin Wall.

Toby and Olivia stood against the Wall, hiding in the shadow. It was well after midnight, and the nearby streetlights provided just enough illumination to make out their outlines. As predicted, the girl appeared exactly at the time specified in Toby's phone call. However, she was alone.

"Where is Leo?" asked Toby.

The girl didn't answer, and then Toby heard a man's voice behind him: Leo's voice.

"Don't look back. Stay exactly where you are now; otherwise I'll shoot you," said Leo. "Tell your partner Zoe to walk out and put her gun down, because she won't be able to see me from where she stands. I assume that you are able to communicate with her via your earpiece."

"I wouldn't be that confident if I were you. I could shoot you right now if I wanted to," Zoe said. "Put your gun down now."

"Take it easy." Leo threw his gun to the ground. "Zoe, remember, there are two of us here, and you are only able to shoot one of us at a time; the other would kill you."

"Let's wait and see, shall we?" said Zoe.

"All right, tell me what you want to talk about." Leo turned to Toby.

Before Toby said anything, Olivia took a few steps forward. "Leo, where have you been all of these years? Why didn't you contact me?"

Toby wanted to say something but ended up with silence. He watched Olivia with a heavy heart.

"Liv, I have been very busy...trying to save the world," said Leo while glancing at Toby.

"But you should at least have told me you were still alive..." Olivia began sobbing uncontrollably.

"Liv, I am so sorry... I missed you so much," said Leo.

"Really?!" Olivia raised her gaze.

Toby sighed inside, almost unable to watch, but he forced his eyes to stay on Leo.

'Yes. I never stopped thinking about you. You know I have to focus on searching for artificial consciousness. We can't let four and a half billion years of evolution vanish from the universe forever." Leo glanced at Toby once more and then continued. "Liv, I still love you. Please forgive me."

"Leo," Olivia cried, and lurched forward; she embraced Leo and kissed him fiercely.

The development shocked everyone.

"Liv!" shouted Zoe, but she didn't say anything after that.

Toby moved his head away from Olivia and Leo, looking at the ugly concrete of the Berlin Wall instead. Nobody knew how many people died trying to scale the Wall to freedom; the great irony was that it was questionable whether anyone had really found any freedom... Just as all sorts of random thoughts floated through Toby's mind, he heard Leo say:

"Toby, Liv told me about Professor Smith's instructions to you. Now you have found me, so what would you like to do next?"

Olivia was still embracing Leo tightly, her face buried in Leo's chest. Toby spoke calmly. "Leo, we all have a common goal: saving human consciousness. That's what we should do next."

"In that case, why don't you come with me so we can find out how to transfer human consciousness? You are the only Taibot with human consciousness; surely you are able to help us to achieve our common goal, right?"

Toby turned around, looking at Zoe, who walked out of her hiding place, then at Olivia and Leo. He finally made up his mind. "I was just a one-off fluke, and Professor Smith has been unable to repeat it since. Are you aware of the imminent methane explosion over the Arctic Circle?"

"Yes, I have been aware of it for a very long time," said Leo. "Based on my calculations, we have at most two days left."

"Two days?" Zoe turned to Toby. "I thought we had a couple more days, based on your calculations."

Toby shook his head. "I did say my prediction was a rough estimate." He turned to Leo. "So we are running out of time. You take Liv to the bunker to continue the research, and here is the software and data from Professor Smith's research."

"You are not going to the bunker?" asked Zoe in a surprised tone.

Toby laughed bitterly. "Zoe, I am only a messenger to pass information to Leo. Have you forgotten already? I am just a Taibot with human consciousness."

168

"Very well, Toby, you have done a great service to humanity," Leo said. "And my personal thanks for delivering Liv to me." He then turned to Zoe. "Zoe, the situation has changed quite dramatically; you see, we are not enemies anymore, as your best friend is with me now."

"Okay?" said Zoe.

"This is what we are going to do next," Leo said. "My Taibot girl will take her gun out to watch over you while Liv and I leave here, just in case you change your mind. Zoe, I am sure you do not want to harm your best friend, right?"

"Liv, do you really want to leave with him? I don't think he is the Leo you knew and loved," said Zoe.

Olivia lifted her head from Leo's chest. "Zoe, he is exactly who I knew and loved. I will go with Leo to wherever he needs to go; I need to follow Professor Smith's instructions and help Leo to save human consciousness."

Zoe wanted to say something, but Toby spoke first. "Zoe, please let them go; they have an important task to do."

Zoe stood beside Toby, watching as Leo and Olivia disappeared into the darkness behind the concrete wall. A few minutes later, Leo's Taibot girl was also gone.

"Toby, I thought you loved Liv. Why did you give up on her so easily?" asked Zoe.

Toby scanned around before he answered Zoe's question. "I do love Liv with my entire life, and that's why I let her go."

"I got it; true love is giving, not taking. Toby, I have to say, you are more human than most humans."

"I am so glad Olivia finally found her true love again," Toby said; however, his facial expression looked a bit strange. Just as Zoe started to ask about it, Toby suddenly said urgently, "Let's get out of here; something is not quite right…"

Even before Toby finished his sentence, figures emerged from the darkness behind and around the Wall; armed men surrounded them.

169

25. Common Goal

Zoe walked to the couch and sat down. "I have to say, it's not very comfortable getting your hands cuffed behind your back."

"I suppose GW learnt their lesson when they didn't handcuff me last time." Toby stood by the window with the heavy curtain drawn closed. They were in a large room, seemingly like a hotel suit. Toby wasn't sure about their location, as they were taken in with bags over their heads.

"Why do you think Leo would betray us?" Zoe asked. "I can't figure out his motives; after all, aren't we supposedly working toward the same common goal?"

"Giving him the benefit of the doubt, I would say Leo doesn't trust you." Toby turned, looking at Zoe. "I think he may suspect you are still working for the government, Australian or US or both."

"But I am a fugitive running from the agency, for God's sake." Zoe stood up, pacing backward and forward a few times. "Okay, let's for argument's sake assume I am still working for the agency: what difference does it make?"

"It seems GW has penetrated the agency quite extensively, so Leo doesn't want to take any chances," Toby said dryly. "Another reason could be that Leo wants to get rid of me. He might be jealous, I suppose."

"Toby, I am sorry to ask this, but as a Taibot, do you have the same emotions as a human? Is your love toward Liv the same as hers toward Leo?"

The same strange expression appeared on Toby's face. "Zoe, I don't know what human love is like. I suppose there is no way one human can be sure about other human's consciousness, and even less so about mine."

Zoe shook her head and sat back on the couch. "I don't think anyone has ever really understood or worked out what consciousness really is. The world is going to end in two days'

170

time, so it doesn't matter anymore." She leaned her head back, resting on the couch for a while, and then spoke with her eyes still closed.

"Toby, are you scared of death?"

Toby walked over and sat on the couch beside Zoe. "Yes, but I am not sure if scared is the right word; I was more concerned about disappearing from existence forever. The whole universe would keep going without me. Each time I thought about it, I felt like I'd been hit by a brick. You know the feeling where there is no second chance; that's it? That type of feeling."

"Fascinating!" Zoe turned her head around, staring at Toby. "A Taibot with human consciousness has the same thoughts and emotions toward death as a human. I have the exact same fear. Toby, you kept using the past tense; does that mean you are no longer afraid of death?"

"Well, after talking to Liv's father about Taoist philosophy recently, my perspective on the universe changed quite a lot."

Zoe sat up, gazing at Toby's eyes. "You are telling me that Taoist philosophy transformed your fear of death?"

"I'm not sure about transformed, but I did a lot of thinking about it."

"I can imagine how much thinking you have done, considering how fast your thinking can be," Zoe said.

"Taoists believe that humans belong to nature, so life and death are just part of the natural process, like day and night, spring and autumn; there is nothing to fear or regret about it. Besides, fear of death is the by-product of consciousness, so when you gain consciousness, you gain fear as well. Like Taoism says, Yin and Yang."

"Wow, a Taibot with human consciousness, and now a Taoist philosopher as well. Fascinating," cried Zoe. "Okay, Toby, you are not scared of death; what about love?"

"What about love?"

171

"I assume you love Liv quite a lot; dare I say, true love. So do you regret losing her, losing your true love forever?" asked Zoe.

"Regret? Oh no, I am lucky to have found my true love, and I feel really happy knowing Liv is in good hands. Zoe, do you have anyone special in your life?"

Zoe hesitated for a second. "I only told Liv about this, but what the heck. You know my Taibot partner, Nick?"

"The one killed in Africa?"

"Yes. We had a good, intimate relationship for quite a while; now, thinking about it, I believe I actually loved him."

Toby nodded.

"Toby, do you think Nick could by chance also have had consciousness?"

"Zoe, I don't think consciousness is unique to human beings; other beings also have their own consciousness, but it is different from humans'. I am quite sure that Nick had his own consciousness, and he definitely loved you in his own way."

"Toby, thank you so much." Zoe couldn't help but start crying.

Toby waited until Zoe stopped sobbing. "Zoe, is that why you called the Taibot Nick in Amsterdam?"

"Yes, he somehow reminded me of my Nick." Zoe leaned her head back against the couch again, closing her eyes. "I am sort of envious of Liv..."

"Liv!" Toby cried loudly.

"What's the matter, Toby?"

"Liv and Leo will never make it to the underground bunker in time," cried Toby.

"You are absolutely right; with GW and the agents hunting them, they won't be able to go anywhere unnoticed."

"There is only one thing we can do: negotiate with GW," said Toby calmly.

"What do you mean negotiate with GW?"

Toby stared at Zoe. "I don't think we have any other choice."

Zoe thought for a second. "Toby, do you really want to see GW's beliefs dominate the post-human world?"

"Zoe, I have looked through human history and found that beliefs have been changing and evolving all the time. It's crucial to keep human consciousness alive; otherwise it will be lost forever."

"Don't you think the universe would be a much better place without human consciousness? Without killing, greed, hunger for power, and ambition; without animal cruelty and the destruction of the natural world?"

"Zoe," Toby said slowly. "Humanity has made mistakes..."

"Mistakes?" Zoe cried. "Humanity is the cause of the sixth mass extinction, right now!"

Toby waited a while until Zoe had calmed down a bit. "I completely agree with your assessment of humanity; however, even if we get rid of human consciousness, how do we know other future intelligent beings will not repeat the same mistakes?"

Zoe thought about it but said nothing.

"So rather than leave it to chance, it'd be much better to keep human consciousness alive, together with the lesson of human failures, so the universe can have a much better future."

Zoe thought for a while. "You are right. Let's get GW..."

"No need," Toby said. "They will walk through that door in two seconds."

"Toby, I am really impressed." A man's voice spoke, and then two men walked in.

"Mr. Logan and Dr. Anderson; I am sure you both quite enjoyed listening to our conversation," said Toby.

"Apologies for our intrusion," said Mr. Logan.

173

"Never mind," Zoe said lightly. "We don't have time for that now."

"So, Toby, what do you want to negotiate with us about?" said Mr. Logan.

"Since you listened to everything we just said, I don't need to repeat myself. Mr. Logan, we need to find Leo and Olivia and escort them to the bunker before it's too late."

"Why would I want to do that? What's in it for me?" said Mr. Logan.

"Well, regardless of our motives, our common goal is to save human consciousness, right?" Toby continued after Mr. Logan nodded. "I was just a one-off fluke, and Professor Smith couldn't repeat the experiment, so the only way to continue the research is to get to the bunker."

"We have our own bunker," said Dr. Anderson.

"I am sure you do." Toby glanced at Zoe and then said, "The bunker not only has all the necessary laboratory equipment for consciousness research, but most importantly it contains the specific hardware that produced me, the only Taibot who has human consciousness."

Mr. Logan and Dr. Anderson exchanged a look with each other but said nothing.

Toby continued. "Time is of the essence. We don't have a lot of time left. Dr. Anderson, I'll download some of the research data from Professor Smith onto your laptop so you can verify that I am telling the truth."

After clicking a few buttons, Dr. Anderson scanned the screen for a few minutes, then looked up at Mr. Logan and nodded.

"Okay, Toby, tell me about your plan," Mr. Logan said.

"This is what we are going to do: I will take you to locate Leo and Olivia, and then we are all going to the underground bunker before the methane explosion wipes every living thing off the surface of the earth," said Toby.

"And you have to promise not to harm anyone; Leo, Olivia, Toby, and I all have to get to the bunker in one piece," Zoe said.

"Of course, all of you are crucial to the success of our common goal," Mr. Logan said. "I want to apologize in advance; I am afraid I can't un-handcuff either of you, just in case you change your mind down the track."

"No need to apologize; we understand totally. Shall we start?" asked Toby.

"Yes, of course." Mr. Logan turned to the door. "I'd like to introduce you to your special escort team leader."

A man walked into the room.

Both Toby and Zoe's jaws dropped to the floor; the man was the Taibot they tried to control in Amsterdam.

26. Refugees

Hamburg was the gateway to Scandinavia, and also the checkpoint for all the European migrants escaping the scorching heat of the Mediterranean in favour of the cooler territory to the north. The armoured military vehicles along the long barbed-wire fences showed how serious the business was.

It was pretty impressive to see the hundreds of checkpoints spread out in the city. Five new train stations had been built for processing migrants. Those specially designed processing train stations/checkpoints formed part of the barrier to stop anyone entering Scandinavia illegally. There was no mercy when illegal migrants were found, and deportation to the south was the only outcome.

Despite everything being so well organized, it seemed like a warzone to Olivia. Migrants carried whatever they were able or allowed to carry with them, jammed into every corner of the city, waiting to be processed. For those lucky ones, they would be on the next train, bus, or ferry to be transferred to the northern parts of Scandinavia, their new home. They would be allocated a spot to settle down in. Unfortunately they wouldn't have the luxury of living together with their countrymen; they would have to mix with migrants from other countries.

Leo gazed at the crowds and the checkpoint in the distance for a moment and turned to Olivia. "Liv, could you please wait for me in that café for a short while; I need to go and find out how to pass these checkpoints."

Olivia nodded. She found that there were quite a few people sitting in the café, so she sat at an empty table next to the window.

"Ma'am, are you by yourself?" asked the waiter.

"Oh no, my husband will join me shortly." Olivia surprised herself with her own words. She didn't know why she called

Leo her husband. After taking her order, the waiter went away, and then a young couple carrying a baby walked in. After surveying the room, they came to the table next to Olivia's. "Ma'am, do you mind if we sit here?" they asked politely in strong French-accented English.

Olivia nodded, so they sat down. "She is so pretty. How old is she?" asked Olivia.

"Eight months," answered the mother. They both had darker skin, seemingly from the Middle East or somewhere around that region.

Olivia noticed their luggage. "Are you heading north?"

"Norway. We are hoping to get to Norway. It is much cooler there," said the husband.

The waiter delivered Olivia's coffee and also took an order from the couple. From the following conversation, Olivia discovered they were from southern France. They were really interested to know what had happened in Australia after she told them she was from down under, so the conversation was relaxing and interesting for all participants.

Suddenly, a group of police officers and armed soldiers rushed in through the front door. "This is a standard ID checking." One of the officers spoke to the crowd.

Olivia knew that Toby had changed their records in the database, so she wasn't really worried. However, she noticed the anxious looks on the couple's faces, particularly the young mother.

It didn't take long for the police to get to their table. Olivia put her wrist up for scanning, and there was no problem, as she anticipated. Then the police scanned the husband—no issue—but the scanner started beeping while scanning the young mother. The faces of the husband and wife changed. The husband hardly managed to form a whole sentence. "Officer, is something…wrong with the scanner?"

The beeping sound attracted a higher ranked officer; he ordered a different policeman to scan the young mother with a different scanner, and the beeping sound continued.

"Ma'am, I am afraid that you will have to come with us," said the officer.

"Please, Officer, our baby needs her mother," begged the husband.

"Sir, this is the law and everyone has to obey," replied the officer.

"But my baby has to have her mother," cried the husband.

"Ma'am, this way please." The officer ignored the husband's pleading.

"My dear, you take our baby; please look after her," cried the young mother while walking out with the police.

"Wait. Officer, I'll go with her, and we'll all live and die together." The husband held their baby, walking out of the café.

Olivia couldn't bear to watch as the young family was put into the police vehicle and driven away, so she stared at her coffee cup until a hand touched her shoulder. It gave her such a shock. Looking up, she saw it was Leo who stood in front of her.

"Why are you crying?" asked Leo while sitting beside Olivia.

She told him about what had just happened.

He thought about it and then said, "I am sorry to hear that..."

"In less than a day, everyone is going to die anyway, so what's the point?" said Olivia quietly.

"Well, think about it." Leo held Olivia's hand. "You can say what's the point to so many things, almost everything we do really."

Olivia raised her gaze. "Leo, that doesn't sound like you."

Leo picked up the coffee cup, sipping a bit. "Not bad."

Olivia drank a bit of hers. "Really? It tastes horrible, nowhere near your standard. Leo, you have changed since the accident."

Leo shook his head. "You are absolutely right. The near-death experience did make me think, a lot actually. I was so passionate about trying to save human consciousness..."

"I thought you were still passionate about it," Olivia interrupted.

"Yes, of course." Leo drank some more of his coffee. "But the more I thought about it, the more I realized that human consciousness is not the only consciousness that exists in the universe."

"I agree with that..." Olivia slowly sipped from her cup. "Leo, human consciousness is the peak of four and a half billion years of evolution, so it's worthwhile to save it, right?"

"Well, the evolution of consciousness is a process. You see, it develops from a single cell to complex life forms, from dinosaurs to humans, and from humans to the next..."

"Do you mean Taibot consciousness?" asked Olivia.

Leo gazed into Olivia's eyes for a second. "I don't know. I think we should get moving. I found a hotel room not far from here. With so many people here, it's very hard to find a room anywhere in the city, so we're lucky to get one."

"Lucky indeed," Olivia said thoughtfully. "Leo, what do we do next?"

"Let's get to our room first and then work out our next move."

"Hi, buddy, what's your name?" Toby asked.

Toby and Zoe were escorted by a team of Taibots and GW soldiers along the streets of Hamburg.

"My name is Nick," said the team leader.

"Really?" shouted both Toby and Zoe at the same time.

"What's the big deal? Why are you both so surprised my name is Nick?" Nick turned around, looking at Toby, then Zoe.

"No way," Zoe said. "I once had a Taibot partner and his name was Nick. When I first saw you, you reminded me of him, and your name is Nick as well. What a coincidence."

"I see," Nick said slowly. "What happened to your partner? Was he decommissioned?"

Zoe nodded. "Yes, he was decommissioned. I miss him so much."

"Sorry to hear that," said Nick.

"Nick, I am impressed GW assigned you, a Taibot, as the team leader of human soldiers." Toby waved his arm at the armed guys around them.

"Well, I suppose GW trust Taibots more than humans. You know, humans can make so many mistakes and have complex motives, but Taibots only focus on their assigned tasks," said Nick in a flat tone.

"You are absolutely right, buddy," said Toby.

"Toby, have you located Leo and Olivia yet? We are getting close to the explosion," said Zoe.

"I know. And the answer is yes," said Toby. He pointed to their left with his chin. "A few blocks that way. They are in a hotel room."

"How can you be so sure? I'd imagine Leo would be quite good at erasing their traces," Zoe asked.

"Yes, Leo is very good at hiding, but I didn't trace them by their presence; I traced their absence. It's called Wu Wei," said Toby.

"Wow, a Taoist philosopher detective," laughed Zoe.

"Nick, tell your men not to kill either Olivia or Leo under any circumstances." Toby turned to the team leader.

"No worries, mate; that's my exact order," said Nick.

27. Hotel

"The hotel on that corner." Toby pointed at a building.

"How many people inside?" Zoe asked.

"Not many. Most of them went out; even they know they will have to wait for much longer, but being near the checkpoints makes them feel closer to escaping the trap inside the city," Toby said.

"So there is nobody else except Leo and Liv inside the building?" Zoe asked.

"A receptionist at the counter and a couple on the top floor," said Toby.

"How do you know all of that?" asked Zoe.

"I analysed the surveillance database," said Toby.

"Of course," said Zoe.

"Nick, Leo already knows we are here, so there will be some shooting; remember, your men can't kill either Olivia or Leo..." Toby said.

"Toby, I know that." Nick withdrew his gun, leading the group into the building.

Nick used his gun, waving it at the receptionist, who understood and ran out the front door immediately. "Toby, which floor are they on?" Nick asked in a low voice.

"Second. Nick, please release us; Zoe and I can deliver Leo to you," Toby said.

"No way." Nick ordered both Zoe and Toby to be handcuffed to the metal pipes near the entrance. A GW soldier guarded them with gun in hand.

Nick led a dozen GW soldiers and Taibots, walking around the counter toward the stairs. Their guns pointed forward, and they proceeded in single file close to the wall.

Suddenly, Nick ducked and rolled sideways. A gunshot sounded, and the soldier next to him fell to the ground. The rest of the team immediately began shooting back. The sound of gunfire filled the hotel hall.

Toby glanced at Zoe, who also scanned around the hall. Then, accompanied by an explosive sound, smoke burst out and filled the hall. It came from outside the hotel, indicating the agents had arrived. Nick's soldiers now had to defend against the newly arrived agents and also continue their attack on Leo.

The GW soldier next to Zoe was distracted by what happened, so he never saw Zoe moving in on him. She slowly lowered her body to the ground, stretched her legs as much as possible, and then kicked at the soldier's stomach; he fell back, landing beside Zoe. Zoe lifted her body up, and her shoulder crushed the soldier's neck.

Amid the thick smoke, Toby was still able to see Zoe as she used her foot, manipulating the soldier's body to get the key. She uncuffed herself, but instead of uncuffing Toby, she picked up the soldier's gun.

Toby watched the action unfurling in front of him in horror.

Olivia heard the gunfire stop. She waited and then slowly walked out from her hiding place. She waited a bit longer and, after hearing nothing, started walking down the stairs.

Dead bodies lay everywhere in the hotel hall.

Olivia scanned the chaos and quickly saw Leo lying in a pool of blood next to the counter. She ran to him and held Leo's hand. "What happened, Leo? Are you okay?"

After a closer look, Olivia saw bullet wounds on Leo's chest and knew there was nothing she could do to help him.

"Liv, I am so glad you are okay…" Leo said.

Olivia looked down at Leo. "Leo, my love, I am okay. Are you hurt badly?"

Olivia then felt a hand touching her arm. She looked up, and it was Toby.

Toby quickly checked Leo and then shook his head at Olivia.

"Liv, please forgive me for taking you away from Toby. I am also a Taibot, similar to Toby... I love you...forever... Please promise me you will go to the bunker with Toby... We both love you..." Leo's head collapsed to the ground.

"Leo," cried Olivia, but Toby held her up. "Liv, we have to go; there are only hours before the explosion. We need to hurry."

With Toby's help, Olivia struggled to stand up and then saw Zoe lying in the corner of the hall, embracing a strange man. She had a gunshot wound on her back.

"Zoe," cried Olivia, but Toby held her tight.

"What happened to Zoe?" Olivia cried.

"Liv, Zoe died trying to save you and Leo. It's a long story, and I will tell you later, but for now we have to go; we don't have much time left."

A bold man walked in the front door. Olivia heard Toby calling him Harry. She vaguely recalled that he was Zoe's boss, but what was he doing here? Toby and Harry exchanged a few sentences, and then Toby said something to her.

"Liv, Harry will use a helicopter to take us to a military base, and then we will use a military plane to parachute to the bunker. I hope we can get there in time," said Toby.

Olivia stared at Toby intensely. "No, Toby, I want to talk to my parents, my family, and say goodbye to them first."

Toby hesitated for a second and then said, "Okay, I will organize the phone calls, but you have to be very brief."

28. Farewell

"Toby, tell me how Zoe died."

They were on a military plane on their way to Norway, where the underground bunker was, based on the information Leo passed to Toby before he died.

"Well," said Toby. It seemed like it was difficult for him to speak; finally he said simply, "Zoe was killed by Taibots and GW soldiers while trying to save you and Leo."

"Where were you?"

"I was handcuffed to a metal pipe, but Zoe managed to kill the guard and free herself."

"Why didn't she free you so you could help?"

"I asked the same question myself, but I don't know the answer. Maybe she was in a hurry and forgot about me, or maybe she was confident she could do it all by herself." Toby sighed heavily.

"How did she get shot in her back?"

"She was shot by a GW soldier. There were too many of them," said Toby.

"Last question: why did Zoe embrace a strange man when she died? Who was he?"

"Do you remember when Zoe and I tried to capture a Taibot in Amsterdam?" Toby continued after Olivia nodded. "By chance, the team leader who escorted Zoe and me was the same Taibot from Amsterdam."

Olivia nodded but said nothing.

"I tried twice to crack the Taibot's code but failed. During the shooting, the Taibot shot Leo, but Leo also got him at the same time. Since the Taibot was fatally wounded, I finally used the opportunity to crack his security code and recover his old memories. You will never believe this: he was Zoe's ex-partner, Nick, who was supposedly killed in Africa."

"What? Do you mean the Taibot was Zoe's Nick, the Nick?" asked Olivia.

"Yes. Unfortunately only in their last minutes were Zoe and Nick able to finally say 'I love you' to each other," Toby said sadly.

"I am so glad Zoe finally found her love, even if it was only for a brief moment," mumbled Olivia. She closed her eyes, leaning against the seat, immersing herself in her own heartbreaking farewell to her family and friends not long ago.

When her face appeared on the fridge's TV screen, her mother got a real shock. It took her a while before she managed to speak. "Liv, where are you?"

"Mum, this is just a quick one to let you know I am okay."

"Ava and Sophie told me what happened at the holiday site…"

"Mum, it'd take too long to explain everything, but I don't have time at the moment. I promise that I'll tell you the details later. Where is Dad?"

"He is at work. Liv, is Toby with you?"

"Yes, he is."

"How lovely. Are you thinking about getting married soon?"

"Mum, it's still too early to talk about that."

"Nonsense. Your father and I will organize an amazing wedding for you. Don't argue with me. We really want to do it for you. When's the last time anyone had a proper wedding?"

Olivia had to pause in order to stop the streaming tears. She finally said, "Thank you so much, Mum. Please tell Dad I love him. I love you all so much. Goodbye and take care, Mum."

"You don't need to be so formal with your own mother. When are you going to come home?"

"Soon. I promise we will meet very soon. Bye, Mum."

The conversation with Ava took place in front of her TV screen in her living room; as it happened, Sophie was there as well.

"Liv, where have you been?" asked Ava.

"What happened to you? Is Zoe with you?" asked Sophie.

"Yes, Zoe is with me, but she is not here at the moment," Olivia said. "Look, I have to run, and this is just a quick buzz to let you guys know we are all safe and sound."

"Liv, tell us what really happened. Both Luke and Michael were killed," said Ava.

"I am sorry to hear that. I promise that I will explain everything to you later, but I have to go now..."

"Wait, Liv, at least tell us if Toby is a Taibot," said Sophie.

Olivia turned around, looking at Toby, who signalled her to stop the conversation; she nodded. "No, he is not. Toby has recovered his memory."

"That's fantastic! Are you coming home soon?" said Ava.

"Very soon, I promise. Goodbye and take care. I love you guys; you are my best friends forever." Olivia hung up without waiting for their reply.

"We have arrived," said Toby.

Olivia blinked her eyes and tried to drag herself back to reality. "Where are we?"

"We are over the highest mountain in Norway. Let's get ready to jump off the plane," Toby said.

Olivia acted like a robot, just letting Toby move her around. She had never been skydiving before, and she could not muster the emotion to feel either scared or excited about the adventure; everything was like a dream, so unreal. Before they were launched into the darkness outside of the plane, Olivia saw a man in military uniform saluting her and Toby. He said something like 'good luck saving human consciousness,' and then she felt herself being swallowed by chilly air and darkness.

Olivia kept her eyes tightly closed. She was quite sure all of this was just a nightmare, and everything would be okay when she opened her eyes tomorrow morning. She didn't know how long it took, but finally they landed on solid ground with a thud. She opened her eyes and found she was on a rocky mountaintop.

It was the middle of the night, and she felt quite chilly on top of the high Norwegian mountains. Olivia could see the white stuff on the ground. Could it be snow? After a close look, she confirmed it was snow.

This must be part of her dream. Otherwise where would the snow come from? She took a handful of snow and cheered. Everything would be all right; it was so exciting. Olivia couldn't remember the last time she saw snow. She danced in the snow, cheering and shouting and singing...

"Liv, I am afraid we have to keep moving." Toby held her hand and pulled her forward.

They walked through the knee-deep snow for a while. There was no light, but the white snow reflecting the starlight was sufficient to illuminate their way. Olivia really enjoyed the coldness on her skin. She didn't know how long they had walked when finally Toby stopped.

"This should be it," Toby said.

They were at the bottom of a cliff; she looked up and saw the rocky wall disappear into the darkness. Toby pushed and knocked around for a while and finally, with some mechanical grinding noises, a large piece of rock sank in, and a door appeared.

"Follow me." Toby led the way and Olivia followed closely. Behind them, the rocky door closed automatically. They were walking inside a narrow, rocky tunnel that had dim electric lights along the way. After a couple of minutes, they arrived at a large hall. There was a car parked at the entrance of another tunnel. Toby climbed into the driver's seat and Olivia got into the passenger seat, and they drove down the tunnel.

Olivia felt that they were zigzagging downward for a very long time. She didn't ask questions, just stared at the tunnel's endless rocky walls under the car's headlights. Finally they stopped.

Olivia had lost track of how long they had been driving. Toby got out of the car and signaled Olivia to follow. With the help of the car headlights, they walked to a large metal gate. Toby pushed a few places on the rocky wall beside the gate, and a piece of rock slid away, a panel with a keyboard appearing underneath.

A smile appeared on Toby's face. "Thank God it works," he mumbled. Toby quickly entered a long series of numbers and letters, and the giant gate slid open.

"Welcome to the last refuge." Toby held Olivia's hand, walking inside the gate.

Dim lights were sparsely placed on the rocky walls. The gate closed behind them. Olivia held onto Toby's arm tightly, looking ahead. She was afraid of entering the unknown. For the first time in her life, she felt her fate was beyond her grasp.

After a few turns and a fair bit of walking, they arrived at another gate. Toby repeated a similar procedure to open the gate, and then they walked along more tunnels. As Olivia was wondering how many of these gates they would have to enter before arriving at their final destination, Toby announced that this would be their last gate, the fifth gate.

The first thing Olivia noticed was that the air smelt much fresher and cleaner; the lights were also brighter compared with the occasional dim light along the long, rocky tunnels. The open space they entered looked like a lab to her. In fact, it was almost identical to the AI lab in Sydney, which she had visited many times while Leo was working there.

"How long before the methane explosion?" asked Olivia.

"Based on the data collected from the Arctic monitoring stations, the methane in the atmosphere has reached the critical point, so it could explode at any moment."

Olivia stared at the glass of water in her hand for a very long time, and suddenly her eyes brightened. "We will survive the explosion, right? Surely there must be hundreds of deep underground bunkers like this around the world, so plenty of people will survive, so humanity will survive, right, Toby?"

Toby stood up, walking away a few paces, and then came slowly back. He looked at Olivia's desperate and hopeful face. "Liv, you are right, there must be many deep underground bunkers like this, and many people will survive the explosion, but for how long?"

"They will have sufficient food and water for years, right?"

"Right. But it'd take millions of years for Earth to regain balance and be suitable for complex life forms to live on again."

Olivia looked at Toby, real fear in her eyes. "Toby, are you saying that this will be the end of humanity?"

Toby sighed. "Not only humanity, but also almost every complex life form on Earth as well."

Olivia laughed bitterly. "The irony is that when humans first came to use their intelligence to create tools, they also sealed their own fate of extinction."

Toby didn't reply.

The ground suddenly shook violently.

"It has started," mumbled Toby.

29. Love

"Toby, I had such a wonderful time with you, and it's been the happiest decade of my whole life; now it's time to say goodbye." Olivia held Toby's neck, kissing him deeply.

The food had run out; the lab was never intended for people to live there for very long without resupplying. The only reason they had been able to live there for ten years was because the food storage was originally designed for a group of staff. Toby had used his resources to search for food on the surface of Earth, but he had found nothing except scorching deserts across all five continents.

Toby didn't know what to say, and Olivia continued. "Toby, do you still remember my reaction after the methane explosion?"

"Yes, how can I forget?" Toby said. "I said to you, 'You haven't eaten for almost a week, and it could damage your health.'"

"And I replied, 'Health? Toby, is there any point talking about health now?'" Olivia said.

Toby shook his head. "I said to you, 'Liv, could you please listen to me: you are everyone's last hope of keeping intelligence going in the universe; please don't let the peak achievement of four and a half billion years of evolution come to nothing.'"

Olivia laughed. "So you managed to persuade me to start eating again. Toby, what are you thinking about now?"

"I am thinking about our attempts and failures in trying to transfer consciousness over the years," said Toby.

Olivia stroked Toby's hair. "Toby, you are always blaming yourself for the failures, but I managed to make you forget about it and enjoy the time we spend just being together."

"Yes, you did, and we spent such a wonderful time together," said Toby.

"Toby, I still remember the first time you transferred yourself into a robot's body."

It was five years since the Arctic methane explosion that destroyed almost all complex lifeforms on Earth. After numerous failed attempts to transfer Olivia's consciousness to computer chips, Toby reluctantly agreed to give up the task. In order to keep the food supplies running a bit longer, Toby organized getting the chips in his head transferred to a robot's body, so he could live on electricity. Toby programmed the details into surgery robots. His Taibot-to-robot transferal operation was a success.

Olivia touched Toby's face. "I know you are inside a robot body, but I can hardly tell the difference, thanks to the advanced artificial skin and robot technology."

Toby smiled, but said nothing.

Olivia thought for a while and said, "Toby, I know we've discussed this so many times over the years, but I'm still unable to figure out how Leo, I mean the Taibot version of Leo, gained human consciousness. It's something I really would like to know before I die."

"I am not sure if I am able to share any new insights on the topic, which we have already discussed many times, as you mentioned. We are still not sure if he did develop his own human consciousness."

"I know it's unlikely we will agree on this, but I am pretty convinced Leo had human consciousness," said Olivia.

Toby shrugged but said nothing.

"Never mind. I suppose if we couldn't work it out in the last ten years, there is much less chance now." Olivia turned her head around and gazed into Toby's eyes.

"Let's assume we had worked out how to transfer human consciousness into a Taibot, and your case was not a one-off fluke. But, Toby, although you have Leo's consciousness and his memories, could we actually claim that Leo hasn't died, rather he just lives inside a different body? In other words, are you 'Leo'?"

Toby sat up, looking down at Olivia, who lay on the platform. "It's a very fundamental question: what defines me as me? Now, since all of my memories have been recovered, each time I think about it, I have no doubt that I have always been 'Leo.'"

Toby stood up, pacing around the platform a few times and then said, "Let me put it this way: you go under general anaesthetic for an operation. When you wake up, how do you know you are still 'you'?"

Olivia sat up. "Because I remember I went into the operation and the injection that put me under. I still have the body I am familiar with; for example, the mole on my left forearm."

"Okay, let's say that the surgeon replaces your left forearm with an artificial one. You know how advanced medical technology can be, so are you still 'you'?"

Olivia thought about it. "An interesting point. I am sure I am still 'me' but with a different forearm."

"Let's go further. Actually, let's go all the way: say the surgeon replaces your body one piece at a time during subsequent operations—your other arm, legs, liver, heart, etc. You know that medical technology is able to do all that quite easily, right?"

Olivia nodded.

"So after all of your body parts have been replaced, are you still 'you'?" asked Toby.

Olivia stood up, looking down at her own body for a few minutes. "Yes, I would say I am still 'me' because I can remember all of those operations."

"Now let's say Professor Smith actually transferred your consciousness and memories to another body, so you should be still 'you,' as you could remember the transferring operation as well, right?"

"I see." Olivia sat down on the platform. "I know where you are going now. So are you telling me there is no real difference between life and death?"

Toby sat beside Olivia. "There is quite an obvious difference when humans only live in their original biological form, but when it's possible to transfer consciousness and memories from one body to another, the boundary between life and death becomes blurrier; in fact, no one could tell the difference anymore."

"Toby, these are very interesting points, and there are certainly so many things to think about, but unfortunately, I've run out of time. Toby, please make love to me for the last time."

Toby felt so sad during their last lovemaking session, but it amazed him that the sadness and hopelessness disappeared from Olivia's eyes for the first time since they came down to this deep underground lab. Toby was really puzzled. After their lovemaking storm passed, Toby asked:

"Liv, you seem enlightened; please tell me why."

"Well, Toby," said Olivia, "death has always been the most difficult question humans have faced since they have been able to think, and that's why all religions and philosophies were created. Unfortunately I am an atheist, so it's double difficult for me to cope." She paused, helping herself to a glass of water, and then continued.

"I was deeply in love with Leo, and I believed he was my only true love, but Toby, in this last moment of my life, I know that I love you, not as a substitute for Leo, but you as Toby. I have found my true love again, and it's you, Toby. I don't care about death anymore, Toby, because now I have you, my true love."

"True love…" Toby murmured, as if lost in some kind of deep thought.

"Toby," Olivia continued, "I always believed that there would be only one true love in my life, so after I lost Leo, I never thought I could fall in love again, but Toby, my love, it's you who brought love to me. Over these years together in this deep underground place, we've had a wonderful life together, but only today did I realize that I truly love you..."

"Only today..." Toby mumbled.

"Yes, Toby." Olivia lay on the surgery platform. "Toby, hold me tight while pushing the button. I want to sleep in your arms forever."

Toby lay beside Olivia, holding her, his right hand hovering over the red button that would end Olivia's life mercifully.

Olivia held on to Toby and kissed him for the last time. "My dearest, my true love, goodbye." Olivia closed her eyes.

Toby suddenly jumped off the platform. "True love, that's it!" He waved his arms, jumping up and down and running around the room.

Olivia sat up. "Toby, tell me what happened."

Toby came back, sitting beside her. "In quantum physics, there is a phenomenon called particle entanglement..."

"I heard Leo talking about it; something about when two particles entangle, they stay entangled regardless of the distance between them, right?"

Toby nodded. "Yes. Throughout history it has puzzled the greatest minds, including Albert Einstein; nobody could come up with a plausible theory to explain it."

"Toby, why are you suddenly talking about quantum physics right as I am going to end my life?"

Toby held Olivia's face and kissed her softly. "My love, you are not going to die. You have solved the last puzzle, the puzzle of consciousness."

"I am not following."

Toby looked into Olivia's eyes, only an inch away. "In almost all cultures, people believe that true love can last forever, even beyond life, time, and space, but no one ever thought to link it to the particle entanglement phenomenon. Love is part of consciousness. If we consider that consciousness is also one of the elemental forces in the universe, alongside others such as gravity and electromagnetics, then true love would explain the particle entanglement phenomenon perfectly."

"I am still not quite following."

"True love is like two particles that are entangled, and the souls or consciousness of the two lovers will remain entangled regardless of the distance and time between them..."

Olivia interrupted. "So the reason Leo's consciousness was transferred into the chips in your head was because of my love for him," said Olivia thoughtfully.

"Exactly! And the subsequent unsuccessful attempts to repeat the same process were also due to the lack of such true love," said Toby.

Olivia's eyes suddenly became bright. "Oh, Toby, my love, you are such a genius."

Olivia lay down on the surgery platform, watching the TV screen above that showed the operation on her brain being carried out. She closed her eyes while the robots wired her head to a robot nearby. Toby stood near her, monitoring each step of the operation closely.

"Liv, open your eyes; this is it," Toby said.

Olivia opened her eyes; there was nothing new on the TV screen above. Her brain was linked to the robot nearby via millions of optical fibre cables. Olivia had provided inputs to the design of the robot; it looked like her, but she had also made some physical modifications. As she watched the TV screen, her vision became blurry.

"Toby, I can't focus; is there something wrong with my eyes?" Olivia said, but it seemed Toby didn't hear her; he was watching the instrument panels intensely.

Olivia felt more anxious as her vision kept getting worse and worse. Finally it was as if she was seeing through a yellowish plastic. She was so frustrated that she used her hands to rub her eyes. It helped; she was able to see again, but what she saw almost gave her a heart attack.

Olivia saw herself lying on the surgery platform with her head wired to somewhere... Following the wires, she decided they were wired to the panel behind her. How could this be possible? She was looking at her own body on the platform.

"Toby, what's happening to me?" Olivia cried out loudly.

Toby, who sat with his back to her, suddenly turned. "Liv, is it you crying?" His voice was filled with anxiety, anticipation, and hope.

"Yes, it is me; tell me what is happening to me," Olivia shouted.

"Please stay where you are; don't move. We are almost done." Toby turned to the robots near the surgery platform.

It was such a weird sensation to watch the robots remove the cable links from the body, her other body, and then from her head, her current head. Only then did she realize what had really happened to her. "Toby, am I living inside a robot's body now?"

"Yes, you are, but please lie still. I need to carry out more tasks to get you sorted completely. Close your eyes and have a long, sweet dream. When you wake up tomorrow morning, you will be in a completely new universe."

After that, Toby pushed a button, and Olivia slowly closed her eyes, with a smile still hanging on the corner of her mouth.

Toby sat beside her, stroking her hair, and sighed. "Liv, my love, that was a wonderful love theory, and I do wish it was true; unfortunately, the reality is quite different. To tell the truth, I would have to start from the beginning."

30. Toby's Story

Professor Smith failed to transfer human consciousness to a Taibot after over two decades of hard research and laboratory experiments. However, he realized that, despite Taibots only possessing certain degrees of consciousness for the time being, it would eventually evolve into human consciousness, although it'd take a very long time. He also believed Taibots would repeat humanity's tragedy in a post-human world, because they would inherit weaknesses, beliefs, and other self-destructive human traits. Witnessing the chaos and suffering during the sixth mass extinction, which was caused by humanity's greed and stupidity, Professor Smith came to the conclusion that the universe would be a much better place without human consciousness.

This deep underground bunker was the last resort to save human consciousness, and it was equipped with the communication capabilities to link to all Taibots around the world.

Professor Smith used his dead son Leo's memories, creating Leo the Taibot to carry out human consciousness research in the bunker after the humans were gone. However, he also secretly made a copy of Leo and called him Toby, so now you know about my origin.

My secret mission was, after humans were gone, to go to the bunker and wipe out all memories, programs, and basically everything from all Taibots' chips, to ensure the total elimination of all artificial intelligence and consciousness.

To ensure the completion of my mission, Professor Smith equipped me with special code-cracking capabilities, so that's how it's so easy for me to break into databases and hack into other Taibots.

Professor Smith saw the methane explosion was coming, and he didn't want to witness humanity's demise, so he organized the accident to kill himself. At the same time, it'd also destroy records and let me slip out without being noticed by the outside world.

It's impossible to delete part of someone's memories without affecting other parts, so Professor Smith inhibited my memories related to you. I am not quite sure why or how, or if it was just pure coincidence that I saw you for the first time that day. Now, thinking about it, the strong emotions inside me must have overcome the inhibitions of my memories, and also, most importantly, triggered my consciousness. In other words, the sight of you created my human consciousness instantly.

During the early stages of consciousness, my memories were still being organized, so it appeared that I had lost my memories. Because it happened just before the underground car park event, we—you and I—assumed my memory loss was due to the injury to the back of my head. I only realized the truth much later, after recovering all of my memories.

I don't know how GW and the others learned of my existence and also assumed I had human consciousness. Of course, since my memories were still being organized, I didn't have a clue what was going on then.

Toby paused, stroking Olivia's hair, and then continued.

When I heard about Taoism from your father for the first time, it was a real eye-opening moment. I didn't understand why there was nothing about it within Leo's memories, considering you were together for quite a while. At the time, I used the Internet to search and gain some information about Taoism, not because I suddenly recovered my memories, as it seemed.

Although Wu Wei and other Taoist concepts were intriguing, I didn't give them too much thought until the weekend retreat at the farmhouse. During the debate about the causes of human extinction, I realized and understood the

198

reasoning behind my mission designed by Professor Smith. It was at that moment that I contemplated whether Taoism could be the answer.

Taoism encourages people to give up material goods and go back to nature, but it's been proved impractical since its conception over two and a half thousand years ago. Although many people did follow Taoist ideas and had fulfilled lives, Taoism never became a dominating social force and influence. My conclusion was that this was due to humanity's biological limitations. Therefore, in a post-human world, Taoism would be the perfect solution for a Taibot society.

As a conscious being, I had the instinct of self-preservation, so I would not carry out Professor Smith's mission to eliminate artificial intelligence; besides, it'd be invaluable to keep the knowledge and lessons from humanity to help future beings and prevent the sixth mass extinction from happening again. It was not artificial intelligence but humanity's faults that caused their own extinction. Humanity was destined to be the stepping stone for the next stage, the man-to-machine evolution.

Toby leaned down to kiss Olivia and then continued.

Leo, I mean Leo the Taibot, must have had a similar experience to mine. When he saw you in the farmhouse, his human consciousness was triggered as a result.

When I saw your devastated mental state after seeing Leo, I decided to tell you about Professor Smith's instruction, the altered one, to give you new hope. I am so glad it worked.

I altered airline passengers' online booking information to send Leo messages and ask for his help; that's how the agents arrested the GW soldiers in Sydney airport just in time, so it was not pure luck.

Leo didn't actively betray Zoe and me to GW. He knew GW was watching him closely, but he managed to hide his whereabouts during our meeting just long enough for you both to escape before GW arrived. He did ask for your forgiveness before his death.

Nick was never destroyed in Africa. Somehow GW obtained him and used his chips to infiltrate the agency's databases. GW then reprogrammed Nick to make him one of their soldiers, but the same thing must have happened to Nick when he saw Zoe in Amsterdam: his consciousness was triggered. Because of his newly gained human consciousness, I was unable to crack his codes and control him. However, Nick's consciousness didn't manage to completely break down his memory inhibition, so he didn't recognize Zoe until the last moment.

Toby hesitated for a few seconds and then continued.

When I was captured by GW, I debated with Zoe whether we would be better off without human consciousness in the post-human world. In order to save you and Leo, I was even prepared to share this bunker with GW. I thought I persuaded Zoe quite successfully, and she agreed with the decision.

During the gun battle in the hotel, Zoe managed to kill the guard and free herself from her handcuffs, but she didn't free me. I was confused initially, but soon I realized the cold reality: after she killed the rest of Nick's team while they exchanged fire with agents outside the hotel, she also shot both Leo and Nick. Then she turned around and pointed her gun at my face. I asked her why, and she said she was protecting the future universe from being destroyed by any intelligence or consciousness.

It's lucky that I managed to crack Nick's codes due to his injury, just in time to reveal to Zoe who Nick the Taibot really was. Nick recovered his memories and recognized Zoe. It's so lovely that they finally said 'I love you' to each other. But Leo somehow didn't die from Zoe's bullets. He shot Zoe from behind.

I didn't blame Zoe for what she did, and I largely agreed with her opinions. If I were in her shoes, I would most likely do the same. It's only a pity that I didn't have an opportunity to explain my idea of using Taoism to solve the problem. I should have been able to detect her real intentions before entering the hotel, but I was too involved with other issues. I am so sorry I didn't manage to save Zoe's life.

Toby lay down beside Olivia and held her tightly.

My initial reason for making up the entangled particle love theory was to make your departure more merciful. However, my dear, although the love theory may not be true, based on Leo's, Nick's, and my own experiences, love did trigger consciousness, so in that sense, you are absolutely right: love is the fundamental force in the universe.

I induced an out-of-body experience to create the illusion that your consciousness had been transferred to a Taibot's body, so when you finally wake up in a new body, you will have the memories of knowing you are still 'you.' As discussed, when it's possible to transfer memories into chips, combining them with a conscious being, the boundary between life and death becomes blurrier. In your new body, you will be the real 'Olivia' in the same way as I am 'Leo.'

Maybe I should have told you the truth before you went to 'sleep,' but it's not necessarily the best thing for you and for the future world. I felt the need to spit it out, even though you wouldn't hear any of it. I will only speak about it this once.

My love, have a very long, sweet sleep. I have so much to do. When you wake up, it'll be a completely new world.

Epilogue

"Time to wake up." Toby spoke softly in Olivia's ear.

Olivia opened her eyes; for a moment she had no idea where she was. Scanning around, she couldn't help but cry. "This is my apartment."

"Yes, it is your apartment." Toby poured her a cup of coffee.

The wonderful smell of strong coffee teased her nostrils; she smiled broadly after a sip of the black liquid. She put the cup down on the bedside table, stretching her arms, feeling wonderful. "You moved me from the underground bunker in Norway to my apartment in Sydney while I was sleeping?"

Toby nodded.

"Thank you so much." Olivia held Toby's neck to kiss him; she felt something different, so she kissed him again and then studied the taste. "Toby, don't tell me that I am kissing a bio-fleshed Toby."

Toby smiled. "You are not wrong; it's a kiss between two human-fleshed lovers."

"Really?" Olivia used her hands, touching her cheeks and then her body. "I got my human body back?"

"Of course. Not only a human body, but a hundred percent matching your own DNA as well."

Olivia thought about it. "Is my consciousness in the chips or in my bio-brain cells?"

"In the chips," Toby said. "Get dressed; I want to show you something."

Olivia stretched her arms again. "You have done so much while I was asleep; how long have I slept?"

"About seven hundred thousand years, give or take a few decades," said Toby casually.

"You are joking, right?"

"I know it's hard to believe. It would have taken tens, even hundreds of millions of years for Earth to regain its ecological

202

balance, but with the help of Taibots, we did it within a few hundred thousand years," Toby said.

Olivia jumped out of her bed, rushing to the window. "Toby, you recreated Sydney?"

"Yes. It's a bit sentimental; a reminder of humanity's contribution to universal intelligence and consciousness," said Toby.

"I'll have a quick shower; I so desperately want to see the new and old city." While walking to the bathroom, Olivia ordered the TV to switch on, and then stopped. "Toby, have you recreated the whole world as it was before the extinction?"

"Well, we thought it'd be fun to live in the olden days again, but we didn't create seven billion people on Earth."

Olivia sat down on her bed again. "Toby, when did you re-introduce all of those plants and animals?"

Toby sat beside Olivia. "We, the Taibots and I, spent the first four hundred thousand years cleaning up the excessive CO_2 from the atmosphere and oceans. As a result, Earth cooled down again. We introduced plants during the next hundred thousand years to make the earth's surface green and also restored balance in the oceans. Only two hundred thousand years ago, we started to reintroduce land animals, and then humans..."

"How did you reintroduce humans?" Olivia interrupted.

"Well, it's actually inaccurate to call it reintroducing humans; humans had gone extinct. What we created were not humans, but the next evolution, combining AI with human bodies, or Taibots with human consciousness. However, we are still calling them humans for convenience, and also to honor our heritage of consciousness and intelligence from humans."

"Okay, not humans, but Taibots with human consciousness," said Olivia. "How did you create their consciousness, so many of them?" Olivia gestured at the news on the TV wall.

"After successfully transferring your consciousness to a robot, the following was relatively easy. By combining your consciousness with mine, AI computers were able to create limitless individual consciousness to fit into the new AI-human bodies that are now living across the globe and beyond."

"I can't wait to go outside." Olivia rushed into the bathroom.

The weather was crisp, cool, and clear. It brought back Olivia's childhood memories; her last memory of weather this cool was back in 2014, when she was six years old. She looked around cheerfully.

"Toby, how were you able to create the streets and building exactly as I remember them?" Olivia turned to Toby, embarrassed. "Forget about it; of course all of this information was stored digitally before the sixth mass extinction."

Olivia was so happy walking along the familiar streets. She waved at the familiar shopping signs and advertisements. The advertisement, a cheerful girl surfing inside a large black coffee cup, was exactly as she remembered when she was ten years old. That advert might have initiated her lifelong addiction to the black liquid. She turned to Toby. "I don't think you had the details needed in your digital database to create this shop."

"You would be surprised to know how much detail we have," smiled Toby.

"You are such a liar." Olivia shook her head, laughing loudly. "Do you know how I know you are lying about it? Because the shop closed two years later, when I was twelve years old. Tell me the truth."

Toby raised his arms. "I give up; I didn't create this shop by following digital information from the database, but rather from your memories. Yes, from your memories. I apologize for intruding on your privacy, but I only accessed the parts strictly necessary."

"No need to apologize." Olivia kissed him while walking. "There is not much in my memories you didn't already know anyway."

Olivia noticed that there were no cars driving on the ground or flying in the air. As she was about to ask, Toby greeted a street cleaner. After they walked around the corner of the street, Olivia asked, "Do you know him? I mean the street cleaner."

"Oh, he is John, just coming back from teaching in a university in Africa for two years."

"Wow, that's quite a life change for him, from a professor to a street cleaner."

Toby nodded. "Liv, look at the brown-haired waiter in that coffee shop. Last year he was a dark-skinned female pop singer ranked in the top ten globally."

"Are you telling me people nowadays can change their gender, jobs, and where they want to live as much as they like?" Olivia scanned the street.

"Of course; people are able to choose whatever they feel like doing and where to live," Toby said. "The most important thing is that people can choose their appearance, their skin, hair and eye colour, their parents, siblings..."

"Hold on, this is a bit too much for me to swallow." Olivia stopped in front of Toby. "Are there any natural-born human beings?"

"The short answer is no. Humans went extinct seven hundred thousand years ago, and we decided it was unethical to reintroduce humans back into this new world."

"Please explain." Olivia noticed people watching them, so she started walking with Toby again.

"Due to their biological nature, humans inevitably carry the associated negative traits, such as greed, hatred, and lust for power, that directly caused the last mass extinction."

"Oh I see, the new humans are perfect because they don't have any of these inherited negative traits. Toby, tell me how the new human society works; who governs them?"

"Liv, do you still remember one of Taoism's fundamental principles: 'the greatest government is no government'?"

"Are you telling me that there is no government in the entire world?"

Toby stopped. "You are absolutely right; there are no governments, laws, rich or poor, wars, racial or gender or age discrimination. People get what they need and do what they are capable of doing. Everything is optimized to reflect the best of each system and each individual..."

"Wow, you have created a utopian society in the real world." Olivia stared at Toby in disbelief. Toby shrugged but said nothing.

Olivia turned around and started walking again. "Toby, it sounds pretty boring to me; everyone is perfect like robots. In fact, they are all robots, aren't they?" She turned, looking at him with a challenging expression.

"No, far from it." Toby shook his head. "All of their consciousness originally came from yours and mine, so each one carries human biological traits, such as desire, pleasure, jealousy, competitiveness, etc. The difference between these new humans and the old biological humans is that they have the ability to control themselves and moderate their desires..."

"Okay, let's talk about your utopia another day. Toby, what would you like to show me?"

They had arrived at the rock area next to the Sydney Harbor Bridge and Sydney Opera House. Toby looked at his watch. "It's the right time."

Olivia noticed large crowds were gathering around them, and everyone was looking at the sky over the Opera House. Just as she was going to ask him what everyone was looking at, Olivia saw a long horizontal white line appeared in mid-air. Then the thin line became thicker, and suddenly, as if a window to another world was opening in mid-air, she saw an alien landscape through the giant window in the sky.

The crowd around her was cheering loudly.

After the cheering died down, Olivia heard cheering from the alien world, and then the view zoomed into a large group of Earth humans; she could tell that the cheering was coming from these humans in another world.

"Toby, please explain."

"Well, it's the greeting from another world on the other side of the Milky Way galaxy."

While watching the images and listening to the voices that took fifty thousand years to reach Earth, Olivia also listened to Toby's explanation of how it had happened. Toby told her that they had sent out millions of Taibots, most of them only with chips and metal bodies to cope with the long journey across the galaxy of up to half a million years. In a similar way to humans walking out of Africa and spreading across the earth, the new Taibots with human consciousness had reached the edge of the Milky Way galaxy.

"That's a wonderful and remarkable achievement, Toby." Olivia hugged him.

The speech from the alien world finished. The speaker put her index and middle fingers together, then saluted the crowds on Earth. "May the TAO be with you!"

The crowd responded in the same way and saluted back. "May the TAO be with you!" And then the sky show finished, and the crowd started to disperse.

"Toby, are they talking about Taoism?"

Toby shook his head. "No. TAO is their religion."

"Oh I see, so what's this TAO religion about?"

"In fact, nobody knows when it started or who started it. You know, every culture has their own creation story, so I suppose TAO is the one for the new humans."

"Do you know what TAO stands for?"

"I heard someone say it stands for 'Totally Awesome Original' but others claim it stands for 'Toby and Olivia.'"

Olivia couldn't believe her ears. She looked around, almost whispering in Toby's ear. "Do they really know the truth? I mean, all of their consciousness originally came from ours and we still live among them?"

"Not sure, but if you ask them, they would all tell you that they were created two hundred thousand years ago in a deep underground bunker in Norway. Anyway, enough about the superstitions of the creation myth. I would like you to meet a few people you will definitely be interested to meet."

Olivia had to put her hands over her mouth to stop the upcoming scream. Not far from them, a group of people had just finished watching the sky show and started walking away. Even from just their backs, she could easily tell who they were. She turned and looked at Toby.

"They were living in your memories, and now they are alive in the real world," Toby said.

"I love you so much." Olivia quickly kissed Toby and then ran to the group.

Toby smiled as he saw Olivia grip one woman from the group by her shoulder and shout, "Zoe, it's me."

Made in the USA
Middletown, DE
24 May 2021